Also Available in the Harlow Cassidy Mystery Series

Pleating for Mercy
A Fitting End
Deadly Patterns
A Killing Notion
A Custom-Fit Crime
A Seamless Murder
Bobbin for Answers
Bodice of Evidence

Praise for the Harlow Cassidy
MAGICAL DRESSMAKING MYSTERY SERIES

TOP PICK
"A charming, whimsical tale that's also chock full of sex, lies, intrigue, and murder...one heckuva series debut. Harlow is a marvelous heroine. Smart, funny, and full of fire. Bourbon's supporting cast is remarkable, as well – a perfect blend of quirk, menace, and heart...the image-conscious, richer-than-God Kincaid family could have been plucked straight from an episode of Dallas; and hunky architect-slash-handyman Will Flores and his young daughter Gracie add heat and warmth (respectively) to the story.

Run to your nearest bookstore and snap up a copy of this whimsical take on a supernatural cozy; you just may find me there standing in line to buy the sequel." **~ The Season for Romance**

"This series debut by Bourbon (who also writes the "Lola Cruz" series under the name Misa Ramirez) has a clever premise, lots of interesting trade secrets, snappy dialog, and the requisite quirky and loveable family. It's very Texas, and

Wendy Lyn Watson fans should enjoy. A fun read with plenty of potential.." ~ **Library Journal**

"A crime-solving ghost and magical charms...a sure winner!" ~ **NY Times Bestselling Author Maggie Sefton**

"A seamless blend of mystery, magic, and dress-making, with a cast of masterfully tailored characters you'll want to visit again and again." ~ **NY Times Bestselling Author, Jennie Bentley**

"Enchanting! Prepare to be spellbound from page one by this well-written and deftly-plotted cozy. It's charming, clever and completely captivating! Fantasy, fashion and a foul play—all sewn together by a wise and witty heroine you'll instantly want as a best friend. Loved it!" ~ **Hank Phillippi Ryan Agatha, Anthony and Macavity winning author**

"Cozy couture! Harlow Jane Cassidy is a tailor-made amateur sleuth. Bourbon stitches together a seamless mystery, adorned with magic, whimsy, and small-town Texas charm." ~ **Wendy Lyn Watson, Author of NAL's Mystery a la Mode series**

"I was really happy and satisfied when I was finished with "Pleating for Mercy" and I want more cozy mysteries like this one." **~ About Happy Books**

"This is a fun read, perfect for vacation or, if you're like me, holed up on your bed turning the pages at 2 AM to find out what happens. I'm looking forward to the next installment in this new series." **~ Stitches and Seams**

"How can you not like a character that can drink a hot cup of Joe as easily on a sweltering day as she can on a chilly 40-degree one and calls herself a "Project Runway," "Dancing with the Stars" and "Iron Chef" kinda gal." **~ AnnArbor.com**

"Pleating for mercy is an engaging novel! It kept me up late, wanting to know how all the details worked out in the end, and making sure my favorite characters were as friendly as I had imagined. I loved how fabric was woven into each part of the story, as the characters weave their own tale." **~ Amy's Creative Side**

"This is the first book in a blissfully enchanting and entertaining series that I hope is here to stay." **~ Notes from Me**

"Harlow is a clever, down-to-earth main character who you can't help but like. Most of the action takes place right in her dress shop, and Harlow asks all the right questions as she tries to figure out the murder mystery....Fans of cozy mysteries will want to be sure to put this one at the top of their "to be read" list." **~ Two Lips Reviews**

"What can I say about this debut series? "Charm"(ing), intriguing, and satisfying; a page-turner with the right touch of potential romance and paranormal just about covers it." **~ Once Upon a Romance**

"This book was a fun read, and the historical tie-in with Butch Cassidy was a kick, as well." **~ Fresh Fiction**

"PLEATING FOR MERCY is a fantastic first book in a new cozy mystery series by Melissa Bourbon. I was quickly absorbed in the book and did not want to put it down!" **~ Book of Secrets**

"This opening act in the new paranormal amateur sleuth A

Dressmaker's Mystery is as enchanting as the magic of the Cassidy women is a two edged sword of both a blessing and a curse. Pleating for Mercy is a spirited whodunit." ~ **The Mystery Gazette**

"Harlow is such an interesting character.I enjoyed this book a lot and felt it was a great first book in a series and sets readers up well for what's to come.Using comic relief to lighten the mood is a common tool employed in cozy mysteries, but I think this one takes it to a new height." ~ **Deb's Book Bag**

"Filled with twists, turns, laughs and mystery, this is a MUST read for that rainy night, that lazy fall day by the fire, or just any time you are looking for a warm, suspenseful, fun read by a wonderful author!" ~ **Reviews by Molly**

"This is the first in A Magical Dressmaking Mystery series, and it is a charming debut. It's full of Texas small town flavor, unique and interesting characters (Grandma the goat whisperer? I love it), good plotting and just enough romance." ~ **Over My Dead Body**

"The book is a blissful read, is suitable for ages preteen, and up, and would make a nice back to school gift for a student or a teacher-but don't forget to buy an extra copy for yourself!" ~ **Myshelf**

"A highly enjoyable paranormal cozy mystery! It would be highly enjoyable no matter the genre label." **~Vixen Books**

"...a good one." ~ **Storybook Reviews**

A Killing Notion

"Talented Harlow Cassidy, descendent of Butch, helps clear a high school football player who's falsely accused of murder in this light paranormal Texas cozy. The series stands at five (after A Custom-Fit Crime); sewing tips and recipes included."
~Library Journal, **April 2014**

4 stars, RT Book Reviews
"Harlow is back and ready to dig into another murder. Bourbon has done a great job with the plot and characters, and the mystery surrounding the murder is fascinating. Readers will find themselves trying to guess what happens, but will end up shocked at the conclusion. With each series installment, Bourbon gets better." *~RT Book Reviews*

4 STARS "This enchanting mystery with down-home charm is as comfortable as slipping into your favorite dress and sitting down and drinking sweet tea with engaging characters who quickly become old friends." ~ The Mystery Reader

"The magic, the mystery, the small town cozy feel, and the nicely balanced mix of characters of all ages make this book a read that promises to entertain those of various generations. It would be a wonderful selection for a mother/daughter book group, a sewing group who likes to read as well, and for those will just plain love the cozy mystery genre...The twist at the end was like the cherry on top of a swirly delicious ice cream on a hot day." ~Laura Hinds

Copyright Melissa Ramirez, 2023

All rights reserved

Cover Design by Mariah Sinclair | www.mariahsinclair.com

Without limiting the rights under copyright reserved above, no part of this publication may be reproduced, stored in or introduced into a retrieval system, or transmitted, in any form, or by any means (electronic, mechanical, photocopying, recording, or otherwise), without the prior written permission of both the copyright owner and the above publisher of this book.

PUBLISHER'S NOTE

This is a work of fiction. Names, characters, places, and incidents either are the product of the author's imagination or are used fictitiously, and any resemblance to actual persons, living or dead, business establishments, events, or locales is entirely coincidental.

The publisher does not have any control over and does not assume any responsibility for author or third-party Web sites or their content.

The scanning, uploading, and distribution of this book via the Internet or via any other means without the permission of the publisher is illegal and punishable by law. Please purchase only authorized electronic editions, and do not participate in or encourage electronic piracy of copyrighted materials. Your support of the author's rights is appreciated.

ISBN: 9798327962262

For Patricia Blandford Liu, because you have become such a lovely presence in my life. I always love seeing your name in my inbox.

Bodice of Evidence

Chapter One

I'd learned over the years that a person is much more than their own history. They are the myth and lore and history of those who came before. For me, that meant I had outlaw in me, courtesy of my great-great-great-granddaddy, Butch Cassidy. Unbeknownst to most people, Butch had fallen in love with my great-great-great-grandmother, Texana Parker. When he left for Argentina with the Sundance Kid, he left behind the love of his life...who also happened to be pregnant with his daughter, Cressida.

Along with his lore and the mythology of the Hole in the Wall Gang, Butch also bestowed on his female descendants a little magic. My great-grandmother, Loretta Mae, always got what she wanted. Before she died, she *decided* she wanted me back home in Bliss, which she artfully orchestrated by introducing me to Will Flores and his daughter, Gracie. That family has its own history of lore and connection to Butch, but that wasn't why I stayed. Will Flores accepted me and my Cassidy charm—unlike my father who'd walked out when he'd found out about my mother's charm.

Our charms had varying degrees of value. Nana was a goat-whisperer. Mama had a magical green thumb. Our family had long tried to fly under the radar, but our magic was more of a don't ask, don't tell kind of thing. People summoned Mama to help with their dying crops. No one seemed to notice or care that she didn't actually have a horticulture background. She fixed things, and that was all that mattered.

Nana's herd, Sundance Kids, could wreak havoc, but those goats produced heavenly cheese. They also provided checks and balances for Mama's green thumb when that green thumb got out of control.

For the longest time, I didn't think I had a charm. But Meemaw knew what she was doing when she brought me back to Bliss. That's when I discovered my magic. I could sew a person's wishes and dreams into a custom garment. It didn't change the world or have a massive impact, but it did affect individual people, and that was enough for me.

What I'd also learned is that my charm might not be enough to keep the doors to Buttons & Bows open—which is why, when someone from the Bliss Arts Center asked if I would teach a course, I jumped up, jolting Josie Kincaid's sweet little nine-month-old baby awake with my scream. "Of course!"

Josie scooped her little girl up in her arms and rocked her back to sleep giving me the stink eye the whole time. "What the heck was that about?" she demanded after I dropped my phone on the table.

"I was just invited to teach a class at the Bliss Arts Center. Fabric painting."

It had taken me only a few minutes to write up the course proposal for the course catalog.

Love sewing? Love painting? Have you ever considered combining these two creative outlets into one stunning creation? Join Harlow Cassidy, owner of Buttons & Bows, Bliss's custom dressmaking shop, and learn how to turn a mundane garment into a one-of-a-kind unique creation in this hands-on class.

"It doesn't sound exciting enough," I said to Josie as she sprawled on the velvet settee—one of the pieces of furniture that had belonged to Meemaw.

I read it over and over, partly to make sure I'd used the right words to describe the class, and partly because I was stalling. After my initial burst of excitement at a little extra cash, I didn't know if I really wanted to give twelve hours of my time over four weeks to a course like this. On top of the time investment, I'd be splitting my course fee with the arts center 50/50. It felt like I was robbing myself of hard-earned money, but then again, I didn't have the room in my little yellow and redbrick farmhouse to teach a sewing class, let alone one that included fabric painting.

Josie cleared her throat. "Earth to Harlow." At the same time, the sound of clanking pipes reverberated from deep inside the walls of the house. Loretta Mae.

"Meemaw," I said under my breath. "Simmer down."

"Read it to me again," Josie said.

So I did, with as much enthusiasm as I could muster. "Love sewing? Love painting? Have you ever considered combining these two creative outlets into one stunning creation? Join Harlow Cassidy, owner of Buttons & Bows, Bliss's custom dressmaking shop, and learn how to turn a mundane garment into a one-of-a-kind unique creation in this hands-on class."

"Former New York fashion designer," Josie said.

"What?"

"Say: Join former New York fashion designer, Harlow Cassidy, etc, etc, etc."

"That's a little self-serving, don't you think?"

She peeked at Molly, sound asleep in her carrier, her fine dark hair pulled up into a thin ponytail on the top of her head. "No, it's absolutely not self-serving. It's the truth. That's what you are. A former New York fashion designer for Maximillian. You should be using that. You're Project Runway—the old one, with Heidi and Tim—meets Butch Cassidy and the Sundance Kid. You're famous in these parts."

I arched a brow at her. "These parts? What, are you living in an old western movie?"

"It's hard not to speak Texan when you grew up and still live in Bliss," she said. "You know it and I know it."

Once again the pipes clanked from the depths of the house as if Meemaw was banging a wrench against them in applause.

They were both right. Since I'd come back my Southern drawl had come back with a vengeance and my wardrobe had picked up a distinct Western flair. "Fine," I said, and added the information.

I read it to her again and she gave her stamp of approval. "Now submit," she said.

That had been a month ago, and now I stood at the front of a classroom in the Arts Center with four women staring at me and waiting for me to teach them how to paint flowers first on the t-shirts they'd brought, then on dresses.

I reviewed their names in my head. Sue Ellen Macaw. Crystal Applegate. Yvette Rodriguez. Mary Lou Pepper. I knew the four were friends and had signed up together. "We've got our thirtieth high school reunion coming up," Sue Ellen had written in response to the welcome email I'd sent. "We're going to wow everyone in the dresses we do!"

So that was my goal. I was going to help these women wow their old high school friends. Of course, I had no idea if my charm of sewing a person's wishes and dreams into a garment so they'd be realized would work if I was painting rather than using a needle and thread. I guess that remained to be seen. I hadn't even known about my charm until I'd come back to Bliss. I'd opened Buttons & Bows when I inherited Meemaw's old farmhouse and since then, I'd been part of the transformation of quite a few Bliss women. I hoped these four would join that elite club. I touched my hairline where a blonde streak grew—a Cassidy trademark that all the women had. When my magic was active, it tingled. Right now, there was not a prickle to be found.

I smiled tightly at the women before me—not because of them, but because of the old schoolhouse desks. This room was *not* going to work. I held up a finger and started for the door. "I'll be right back," I said. I heard them whispering behind me as I scooted out and hurried through the maze of a building until I found the front desk. A woman with short spiky hair sat there scrolling through something on the laptop computer in front of her. Instantly, I saw a vision of an outfit in my head. It was black and white polka dots, geometric shapes, or maybe stripes. I wasn't sure, but whatever the pattern, the high contrast went with her style. Her desk space was neatly organized, but personalized with photographs of what I assumed were family members—maybe kids and even a grandchild, others of her with friends, and one poignant frame of a handsome young man on one side, a poem written in calligraphy on the other:

> *Those we love don't go away,*
> *They walk beside us every day.*
> *Unseen, unheard but always near,*
> *Still loved, still missed, and always dear.*

My thoughts instantly went to Meemaw. The words expressed my sentiment exactly. I couldn't see her, but she was always near. Much more so than this woman—Tawny McVie, her name tag said—had with the loss of this man. She looked up from the magazine she'd been flipping through as I approached, brows raised expectantly, registering where my gaze had settled. "My brother," she said. "We lost him really young."

"I'm so sorry," I said, knowing the words were inadequate.

She smiled. "It was a long time ago. Can I help you?"

From afar, I'd placed her in her late twenties or maybe early thirties, but up close I could see she was firmly in her mid-forties. Crow's feet sprouted from the outer corners of her eyes and fine lines ran like caterpillar hair across her upper lip. She might even be knocking on fifty's door. Her trendy haircut made her look younger than her years.

"Hi, yeah, um, I'm teaching the garment painting class? But the room is not going to work. There's no water source. And we need tables to lay the garments on, not those little desks. I mean *little* desks." I emphasized little the second time in hopes she'd get my meaning—which was that not all the ladies actually fit in them comfortably because they weren't children.

Tawny hopped up with the energy of a teenager. "Oh! Gotcha. Let me see what I can do." She pressed a few buttons on her cell phone and a few seconds later she was speaking with someone, explaining the situation. She listened, nodding, then said, "Gotcha," again and hung up. She hurried around the desk and around the corner until she was on my side of the counter. "I should be able to move y'all to a different space."

She headed back toward the classroom I'd been assigned at a breakneck speed. I scurried to keep up. She stopped at the threshold, interrupting the conversation the women were having about Dairy Queen ice cream and bellowed, "Ladies! Get your stuff and come with me!"

The women looked from Tawny to me. "We're moving classrooms," I said, hoping that wherever Tawny took us would be better than this one. I skirted around her and started to pack up all the supplies I'd brought with me. It would take two trips because teaching an art class required tons of stuff to lug around.

We all followed Tawny through the Black Box Theatre and deep into the bowels of the Arts Center. She flipped a switch to illuminate the dark hallway as one of the women emitted a spooky ghost sound. "Sue Ellen, stop that!" Crystal said. Tawny chuckled as she opened the door to an even darker classroom and flipped on the light.

One by one, we stepped into the new classroom. It had heavy wooden tables rather than small desks, which was good. The tops were covered in paint spatters and pockmarks, the scars in the wood documenting several decades of use. Tawny turned to me. "Better?"

I didn't like being in the caverns of the building, but the space would work much better for the class compared to the other room. "Better," I said. "Y'all, I'll be right back. I need to grab the rest of my stuff." I dug out several long sheets of heavy plastic from one of the bags I'd brought with me and handed them each one. "Lay out your garments and slip the plastic inside," I directed. "I'll be right back."

"I'll help you," Tawny said, and a few minutes later, we were lugging the bags of paints and brushes, the reference magazines I'd brought, transfer paper, and a few sewing supplies, just in case anyone needed anything done to their garments, to the new classroom space. The women were in full gossip mode by the time we got back. "Good thing he never cheated on me, or I'd've pulled a Carrie Underwood on him," Sue Ellen said, wiggling her fingers as if she were casting a spell.

"Which one, Before He Cheats or Black Cadillac?"

A chorus of laughing voices rang out. "Black Cadillac!"

"Maybe both," Mary Lou said. "If someone cheated on

me, I'd take a Louisville Slugger to his car and then I'd do the whole Black Cadillac thing."

"Right, and then I'd bury him out on the ranch with the daisies. At least somethin' good could come of the lying, cheating bast—"

"Sue!" Mary Lou's horrified voice stopped her sister. Sue Ellen's eyes went wide at her bad manners. For a second she looked like she'd seen a ghost, but Meemaw was at home, and the moment passed. A split second later, Sue Ellen burst into laughter. It was infectious and before long, we were all bellylaughing with her, even Mary Lou. "Okay," she said once she caught her breath. "Well bury *me* out with the daisies where I'll never be alone, then. I'll always have my flowers."

As I unpacked my supplies, Tawny walked around looking at what they planned to paint. She made small talk with them, asking them about their families. "Three grown kids?" she said to Crystal. "You do not look old enough."

Crystal flushed. "Bless your heart."

"It's true."

"I have two," Sue Ellen said.

"That's so great," she said, and then she cleared her throat. "Hey, y'all. I'm Tawny McVie. I'm the assistant director here. Just holler if you need anything, okay?"

I thanked her as I finished unpacking my bags. Tawny started toward the door but stopped at Crystal's table. Tawny said something that made Crystal laugh. Then she moved on to Sue Ellen's table. Sue Ellen looked up at her but at the same time, she seemed to slip away into another place. Her face suddenly went pale for a second and her hand went to her heart. Tawny reached for her. "Hey, are you okay? Should I call 911?"

The question broke through and Sue Ellen blinked. Nodded. "Yes. Yeah. Sorry. I just…I just…" She waved her away. "I'm fine. Fine."

Tawny looked unsure. She absently fiddled with her name tag, sneaking another concerned look at Sue Ellen. Finally, though, she started to the door again. "I should get back," she said. "Let me know if you need anything else."

"Sure will. Thanks again," I said. "Thanks for the help."

As she left, my gaze scanned the room. Crystal and Yvette were both organizing their supplies. Mary Lou had moved to her sister's side. They whispered, and then Sue Ellen nodded and I sighed in relief. Whatever episode she'd just experienced, it was over. Phew.

Chapter Two

During the first class session, I had miscalculated the time it would take to teach people to paint on fabric. Actually, I'd started with a completely false assumption. See, I'd assumed that the people who signed up for my class would come in with some prior knowledge, but boy oh boy was I wrong. "I've never even held a paintbrush," Yvette said, frowning.

"Pshaw!" Sue Ellen said, fluttering a hand in Yvette's general direction. Her bottle-blonde hair, cut in the quintessential Texas bob with the hair hitting below the chin and the neckline in back, was a sharp contrast to the bit of dirt stuck under her fingernails. I had paint under mine. Our hands couldn't hide our hobbies. It looked like Sue Ellen liked gardening and I had been immersing myself in fabric paint. "With the way you decorate those cakes, you'll be able to paint a few little flowers easy peasy," Sue Ellen told Yvette.

I looked at Yvette's hands. Faint smears of red and blue marked the sides of her fingers from food coloring, I thought. Only Crystal and Mary Lou's hands didn't reveal anything about their pastimes.

"My first attempt at painting fabric was on the back of a

jean jacket," I said. "I used to love Toby Keith. He was playing a concert in Fort Worth and I talked a friend into going with me. I had to show Toby how much I adored him so—"

Crystal squealed, bouncing in her chair. "Oh my heavens, don't tell me, don't tell me!"

Sue Ellen swung her gaze from Crystal to me, and back. "What? Don't tell you what?"

But Crystal ignored Sue Ellen. "You did, didn't you?'

I nodded sheepishly. "I did."

"What?" Sue Ellen demanded. "What did you do?"

Mary Lou chuckled. "She painted him on the jacket," she told her sister, then looked to me for confirmation, eyebrows raised. "Right?"

"I did. Toby Keith's face emblazoned in acrylic paint on the back of my jean jacket." I felt heat rise to my cheeks at the memory. I tried to imagine my kin, Libby Allen or Will's daughter, Gracie, doing something like that. What singer did they love enough to paint on a piece of clothing? And then it came to me. Taylor Swift. Libby was a Swiftie, which meant she was part of the superstar's massive fandom, replete with a Swiftie bracelet and ID on the Taylor Swift dot net fandom site, and she was in regular communication with other Swifties. Taylor Swift's face could definitely end up on the back of one of Libby's jackets. Who knew, maybe it already had. "Cowboy hat and all," I said, confirming Crystal's and Mary Lou's guesses.

Yvette gave a sideways grin. "Do you still have it?"

That was a good question. I thought it might be packed away in a box in my attic amidst the other things Loretta Mae had tucked away up there. "I'm not sure," I said. "Maybe."

Sue Ellen pshaw'd this time. "Toby Keith? He's got nothing on Willie or Waylon or George."

"Oh no, Kris Kristofferson," Mary Lou cooed.

They were talking about a whole 'nother generation of

country music's bad boys, but I left it. People liked who they liked and who was I to disagree with them? When I looked at Will Flores, I saw a mix of Toby, Tim McGraw, and a touch of Pancho Villa thrown in. The goatee. The rascally gleam in his eyes. The perfect brown skin. Mmm. I glanced at the time on my cell phone wondering when class was over so I could hightail it home because there was a good chance Will would be there.

I pushed that thought aside so I could focus on the class. As the women had walked in, as so often happened, I got quick flashes of garments I'd like to make for each of them. Mary Lou looked comfortable, but basic with her beige pants, slip-on canvas shoes, and A&M t-shirt. I saw her in a white dress with a full skirt. Very retro. Very Marilyn Monroe.

Yvette carried herself with a little more style, but she could use a little update to bring her into the current decade. Her capri pants were too long on her and I had an image of them cut shorter and frayed along the edges. Crystal's personality was colorful, but her clothing lacked that charisma. I could see her rocking something in the style of a Johnny Was floral tunic and one of his colorful embroidered bags.

And then there was Sue Ellen. Like her sister, she was casual. In my mind's eye, she stayed that way, as if this was how she was most comfortable.

But these women weren't in my atelier, which was really just the farmhouse's dining room that I'd converted into my workspace. They were at the Bliss Arts Center wanting to paint t-shirts and then dresses, so I pushed aside my makeover ideas for the four friends and got to work on the business at hand. "Tell me, what brings you to this class?"

Crystal's hand shot up. "I'll tell you why I'm here. I have three dresses that are, shall we say, a little worse for wear? But they have a little life left in them so I thought I could salvage them. There was this *Project Runway* episode where one of the designers used paint to make one-of-a-kind fabric and I thought, *I can do that.* So here I am."

There had been a couple of designers on the Heidi Klum/Tim Gunn show who had used paint to customize fabric. My mind was suddenly filled with images of splashes of color and crazy shapes. "We can have fun with that," I said.

"I'm here because Crystal dragged me here," Sue Ellen said, but she winked so I knew she wasn't salty about it.

"That's because all you do is garden. You need to get out more."

Sue Ellen shrugged. "I don't know why if I love it, but I'm here and I'm willing to try. Also, you have a reputation," she said looking at me. "I wanted to meet the famous Harlow Cassidy."

I felt a burst of heat spread over my cheeks. I would never be well-known like Maximillian, the New York fashion designer I'd worked for, but then again, I didn't want to be like him. Being known for my designs in Bliss was enough fame for me. "I'd love to make y'all dresses one day—"

"That's not what I mean," Sue Ellen said. "You've solved crimes! I've read about you in the paper. I wanted to meet you. I think it's so interesting, your fight for justice. Helping the police solve crimes. I really want to know more."

"That was pure luck," I said, dismissing the praise. Most people never saw a single murder in their lives. I'd seen far too many, and if I never saw another one, I'd be happy. I nodded to the white t-shirt laid out on the table in front of her. "Do you know what you want to paint on it?"

She ran her hand over it. "Flowers," she said.

The other three women groaned. "Flowers, flowers, flowers."

Sue Ellen smiled. "Exactly. It's not like I'm going to paint an oil derrick, that's for sure."

"You could," Yvette said, "but it would not look too nice, I think."

I thought she was right about that. "Daisies it is. How about you, Yvette?"

Yvette shrugged. She placed her hands in the center of the dress she'd brought and moved them away from each other as if she were flattening out the wrinkles. "I don't know," she said.

"It's okay. We'll figure it out," I said, then looked at Mary Lou. "And you? Do you have an idea?"

"I guess I'll do flowers, too. Yellow roses." She looked at Sue Ellen. "Remember that climbing rose bush we had by the front door?"

Her sister closed her eyes for a second as she gave a reverent smile. "Mama loved that. She didn't think that thing would ever bloom, then one year it had a handful, and then—"

Mary Lou clapped her hands and we all jumped. "Then there were hundreds. The thing exploded with 'em."

"I know! I'm going abstract," Yvette said, then she nodded and ran her index finger along the seam that connected the bodice to the skirt of the dress she'd brought. "It'll be like wearing a Jackson Pollock."

I liked the sound of all their plans, but it didn't take long to determine that the four women didn't actually know the first thing about painting, let alone painting on fabric. "Ladies, let's put the dresses away and back up the truck. We need to start with the t-shirts y'all brought."

"Good!" Sue Ellen gave a light laugh. "Because I'm telling you, this is way outside my comfort zone and I really want to get this right. I can't paint a lick, so I don't know what I was thinking takin' this class, and now I have grand ideas and no way to execute 'em."

Mary Lou slapped her hand on her table with a bang. We all jumped and stared. "Don't you do that, Sue Ellen.

You've done some incredible things. Again, look at your gardens."

Crystal and Yvette nodded enthusiastically. "The daisy bed?" Crystal said with reverence. "They're incredible."

Sue Ellen blew a raspberry. "That area is meant for those daisies," she said with the ghost of a smile. "Nothing else will ever go there."

"It will when we sell," Mary Lou said.

Sue Ellen shot her a look. "I'm not selling."

"Someday," Mary Lou amended.

"The ranch needs to stay in the family. I don't want anyone tearing up that yard. Changing things. Digging up everything we planted there."

"They won't, Sue—" Mary Lou started, but she broke off when Sue Ellen held up her hand. "I really don't want to talk about it anymore, okay?"

Mary Lou shrugged and smiled. "Let's paint, then," she said, and Sue Ellen nodded. "Let's paint."

I spent the next thirty minutes demonstrating how to paint a daisy on a piece of muslin, figuring daisies were a little easier than roses, which would rely heavily on shading. Three hours passed in the blink of an eye. By the time we were done, my first set of Arts Center fabric painting students each cradled their muslin daisies as if they were new pairs of Frye boots. "Roses next time!"

They all packed up their supplies and headed out. Mary Lou carried her water bottle. Sue Ellen lugged her heavy tote, a sheet of paper with one of her drawings in one hand. Crystal and Yvette brought up the rear, laughing at their mediocre art skills. Their voices carried as they walked down the hallway toward the building's entrance. "Flowers," Sue Ellen said. "Flowers make even the intolerable tolerable."

"She is right," Yvette said.

Crystal said something that left them cackling like a coven

of witches around a cauldron. Sue Ellen stopped for a second at the front desk and picked up one of the Arts Center's printed class schedules. "Bye ladies," Tawny said, waving as they left. Their voices faded away as they left the building. They reminded me of the Cassidy women when we got together. I also had it with Josie Kincaid, née Sandoval, Orphie Cates, Madelyn Brighton, and even Gracie. I loved that Sue Ellen, Crystal, Yvette, and Mary Lou were so connected because finding that level of comfort wasn't always easy.

Chapter Three

After walking the women out, I went back to the classroom to gather my things. Tawny appeared in the doorway. "Need any help packing up?"

"I won't turn down an offer like that. I brought way too much stuff." Packing it up into the totes was like piecing together a puzzle. I rearranged until it all fit again, making a mental note to remember how to do it next time, and together, Tawny and I made our way back through the halls of the Arts Center. Outside, Sue Ellen, Crystal, Yvette, and Mary Lou had gathered around a big white double-cab pickup truck, their laughter carrying through the parking lot. At Buttercup, Meemaw's old pickup that I'd inherited right along with her house—which had actually been mine since the day I was born—I yanked the passenger door open. It emitted a shrill creak. I put my tote bags in and turned to grab the ones Tawny held. As I got in the truck, she started through the parking lot, heading back to the Arts Center. I cranked down the window as I backed Buttercup out of the parking space, waving to her. "Thanks! See you Thurs—"

A ragged scream cut through the air. I slammed on the

brake, careening my head around to see where it had come from. And then I pinpointed the sound as coming from my students. I pressed the gas and the truck lurched forward into the parking space again. I threw it into park, snatched the keys from the ignition, and practically fell as I hurled myself from the cab. Tawny was already running toward the group of women. She skidded to a stop and I pulled up short behind her. Mary Lou and Yvette were both on their knees and Crystal stood off to the side, her hands visibly shaking. That's when I saw the body.

Not just *a* body. It was Sue Ellen, splayed out on the ground. Her things were scattered around her and one hand clawed at her chest. We gathered around, helpless as I dialed 911 on my cell. Sue Ellen lifted her head and mumbled something. "Mar—"

Mary Lou leaned in. "I have to tell..."

Mary Lou gently touched her sister's lips with one finger. "Shhhh. I'll tell the kids."

Sue Ellen nodded. Her eyelids fluttered then closed.

In the minutes before the paramedics arrived, the crowd around Sue Ellen grew, and lookie-loos gathered on the sidewalk. The crowd parted as the fire truck and the ambulance arrived, tires screeching, sirens screaming. Mary Lou had one fist pressed against her contorted mouth. "*Ohmygod, ohmygod, ohmygod.*" She repeated the slurred words over and over. Crystal stood on one side of Mary Lou and wrapped her arm around her shoulder. Yvette stood a little off to one side, her eyes glassy, lips pressed tight, the tip of her nose tinged red. I moved to her side. "What happened?" I asked.

Yvette shook her head like she couldn't believe it. "We were just talking. Laughing. Like always, and then Sue Ellen got a funny look on her face and put her hand on her chest. Then she fell."

I remembered Sue Ellen putting her hand to her heart

earlier. A heart attack, I thought. The brace the medics had placed around Sue Ellen's neck also made sense now. So did the matted blood on one side of her head. She'd hit the asphalt hard when she'd gone down. The paramedics worked quickly, moving her onto a gurney, stabilizing her with oxygen, and sliding her into the back of the ambulance. One of the EMTs guided the gurney into the back and helped Mary Lou climb in after. Before the doors of the emergency vehicle closed, I saw Mary Lou take her sister's hand, and hold it to her heart. She was keeping it together pretty well, I thought. For a second, I put myself in Mary Lou's place. What if something like this happened to Red? I'd be a wreck, collapsed over him, sobbing. Other than a parent, a sibling was the person you shared the most history with. They usually knew you longer than anyone else, and with an intimacy that came only from sharing a family life. My brother had a wife and kids. He was busy with his own life, but still, I couldn't imagine losing him. The hole left behind would be cavernous.

I hoped Sue Ellen would be okay, and for Mary Lou's sake, I hoped she wouldn't have to suffer a loss of that magnitude.

Crystal, Yvette, and I followed the ambulance in our own vehicles, reconvening in the hospital's waiting room. A young woman in her late teens or early twenties and a young man who looked to be a year or so younger rushed in. Sue Ellen's children, I guessed. Crystal surged toward them, spreading her arms wide and gathering them into an embrace. The teenage boy spoke first. "What happened?"

Crystal gave a final squeeze and released them, stepping back so she could look at them straight on. "Oh my darlings," she said. "We don't have any details yet."

The girl pressed her palm over her mouth, her eyes wide. "They said it was a heart attack?"

Crystal nodded. "That's what we heard."

"Hasn't the doctor been in?" the boy asked. "No updates? Where is she?"

Crystal patted the air to slow his questions. "Your aunt is with her," she said. "They'll come in just as soon as they can."

A gulping sob escaped from the girl and my heart ached for her. I touched the engagement ring on my left ring finger and couldn't help but think of Gracie. Will and I hadn't set a date for the wedding, but whenever that happened, she'd become my stepdaughter. She felt things deeply, and that didn't include the magic that ran through her veins. If something ever happened to Will, I couldn't even imagine the grief that would course through her. A shudder washed over me in a torrent at the very thought.

Crystal guided Sue Ellen's children to three chairs where they huddled together and spoke in hushed tones.

Next to me, Yvette tsk'd quietly. "Poor kids. First the divorce and now this. Life isn't fair, is it?"

She spun around as a baritone voice came from behind us. "Bobby. Madison. Come on, let's go."

Yvette and I turned. A stocky man with weighty jowls that pulled his face down stood rooted to the ground as if he were incapable of actually taking another step...as if whatever happened in the waiting room was contagious.

"That's him. Sue Ellen's ex."

The man looked haggard with puffy dark circles underneath his red-rimmed eyes. If what Yvette said was true, the grief-stricken way he looked wasn't because his ex-wife had nearly died.

Sue Ellen's kids—who I now knew were named Bobby and Madison—left Crystal and hurried across the waiting room. Their dad stepped back as they approached, drawing them around a corner and out of sight.

Not ten seconds later, raised, angry voices came from the

same direction. "How dare you come here," one of them said. I instantly recognized it as Mary Lou's.

"I'm just picking up my kids," the man said.

"Wow." Mary Lou spit out a sarcastic laugh. "She was your wife, Bennett. The mother of your children. Don't you want to know how she's doing?"

"Auntie!" Madison's voice was ragged. "Please don't..."

Sue Ellen's ex, Bennett, and Mary Lou's angry voices faded away. Good. They'd taken their argument out of earshot. Everyone else didn't need to hear their dirty laundry. Bobby and Madison came back in. Madison tried to be stoic but her chin quivered and her tears fell. Bobby's face had turned beet red. He dragged the back of his hand under his nose and sniffed up his quiet sob.

A moment later, a doctor walked in wearing blue scrubs and black Crocs, her hair pulled into a loose bun. She scanned the room. "Sue Ellen Macaw's family?"

Crystal and Yvette surged toward her. "Right here," Crystal said. "Is she going to be okay?"

"For now, she's stable. We're moving her to a room for observation. I'll have a nurse come get you when she's settled. You'll be able to visit her one at a time."

As the doctor left, Bobby's tears sprung forth like a geyser. He and Madison hung on to each other in a tight hug, each of their chins resting on the other's shoulder. The only thought that passed through my mind at that moment was how relieved I was that these two were going to get more time with their mom.

Chapter Four

In the time Sue Ellen had been taking my fabric painting class at the Arts Center, I'd gotten to know and like her. I waited at the hospital, not quite ready to leave, and I soaked in the good news as each person who went in to visit Sue Ellen reported back. *"She has pink in her cheeks!"* Madison exclaimed. *"She smiled at me,"* Bobby said. Crystal gave her own smile. *"She squeezed my hand,"* she said.

I wanted to hear each detail. Yvette came back from her visit, happy tears in her eyes. Mary Lou followed saying "She wants to see you, Harlow."

I hadn't expected that. I pressed my palm to my chest, my eyes opening wide. "Me?"

Mary Lou gestured with her arm. "Come on with me."

I followed her down one hall which led to another and then to another. Finally, we came to Sue Ellen's room. A metal track was mounted to the ceiling around the two beds. Curtains hung from hooks to provide privacy. The first bed was shrouded. In the next bed lay Sue Ellen, a nasal cannula pumping oxygen, tubing running from the IV in her hand to the bag hanging from a stand. She slowly turned her head and

I saw everything the others had reported: pink cheeks, a thin smile, and relief in her eyes that she was alive.

"Harlow," she said. Her voice came out scratchy and hoarse.

I rushed forward. "Sue Ellen, I'm so glad you're okay."

Her smile crept up on one side. "That's what they tell me."

A nurse stopped at the open door and beckoned to Mary Lou. "If I can talk to you for a minute."

Mary Lou hesitated, but Sue Ellen wiggled her fingers—just barely. "I'll be fine."

To me, the nurse said, "Five minutes, okay? Sue Ellen? You need to rest."

"Yes, ma'am," Sue Ellen said, and the nurse and Mary Lou disappeared into the hallway.

"I won't stay. I'm just glad I got to see you—"

"Harlow—" She stopped. Cleared her throat. Started again. "When I'm released, I want to...to talk to you about something."

Usually, when people said something like this to me, it was about wanting a custom dress, but I couldn't picture Sue Ellen in anything right now. Her in a hospital gown overpowered anything else my charm wanted to summon up. "Of course," I said.

"It's...I've got to make..." She trailed off, exhaustion draining what little color she had from her face. "I'm so tired... Tomorrow, okay? I just...can't leave it like it is."

"Leave what?" I asked.

"Tomorrow," she rasped.

Maybe she was talking about one of her fabric painting projects. Oh, lord, this wasn't a death wish, was it? The doctor had told us she'd recover, but Sue Ellen had to keep the faith. Attitude was everything. "Absolutely. We'll talk about it when you're back home," I said, throwing a healthy dollop of cheer into my voice.

She wiggled those fingers again and managed a sleepy smile. "Let's hope for tomorrow," she said. "I might just have to leave on my own..."

"Don't you dare!" I said. "You'll be home soon enough."

She let her head sink into her pillow, her lips curving upward again. "Thank you, sugar," she said. Her eyelids fluttered closed. I waited until her breathing grew steady.

"You're welcome, Sue Ellen," I whispered.

∼

Something jolted me from a deep sleep. My eyes flew open and I tried to blink away the grogginess that had me bound in a cocoon. The phone rang. So *that* was what awakened me. I reached for the old rotary phone sitting on my nightstand. I hadn't been able to bring myself to cancel Meemaw's landline, so most people in town had that number. Not many people actually used my cellphone, which was exactly the opposite of how it probably was for most people...if they even had landlines anymore.

"'Llo?" I asked, my sleepy voice cutting off half the word. I rubbed the blurriness from my eyes with my thumb and forefinger and registered the time. Five-thirty. My heart skittered. It was far too early for any normal person to be calling for any normal reason, which meant something was wrong.

"Harlow?"

"*Gavin?*" Now my heart did a triple flip. Any phone call early in the morning was concerning. One from the deputy sheriff—and my new stepbrother—was downright alarming. My voice cleared and I was instantly alert. "What's goin' on? Is Mama okay? Hoss?"

"They're fine," he said, then he cut right to the chase. "Sue Ellen Macaw is dead."

I pulled the phone away and stared at it as if it had betrayed me. "I'm sorry, what did you say?"

"You heard me right. Sue Ellen Macaw is dead."

"But...but...no. That can't be right. I just saw her last night. I mean, I know it was a heart attack, but the doctor said she'd be okay."

"Well, she's pretty far from bein' okay," Gavin said dryly.

If she was dead, that was a massive understatement. "Do you want me to do something?" I asked, genuinely curious. I wasn't Sue Ellen's family. I didn't even know her very well.

He sighed, the heaviness of it traveling through the phone line. "Her daughter found her at home this morning on her bed. Looks like she died in her sleep."

The words and the meaning behind them hit me like a punch to the gut, but my brain hitched on the details as if they could prove him wrong. "You mean her hospital bed, right?"

"No. At her home."

"But...no. She's in the hospital."

"No. She left."

"I don't understand. There's no way they would have discharged her." Heck, she could barely keep her eyes open when I'd been there.

Gavin threw out another sigh. "She wasn't discharged, Harlow. She walked out on her own."

I let this news sink in. "She walked out on her own."

"Why're you repeatin' everythin' I say? Yes, she walked out on her own. Against doctor's orders."

"In her hospital gown?"

"Yup."

I tried to imagine the scene in my mind. Sue Ellen ripping out her IV and nasal cannula. Slipping out of bed. Walking out of her room and down the hallway. Had she been nonchalant or furtive? Had she taken the elevator or the stairs? "No one tried to stop her?"

I could almost feel Gavin shrug on the other end of the line. "No one saw her go. There's video, which we've already reviewed. It shows her getting into a small sedan. She used her phone app and schedule a ride."

And she'd gone home. That made no sense. "Did she have another heart attack? Is that what she died from?"

"That's my guess."

"Dead," I muttered.

"Dead," he confirmed.

Good God, how I wished I could erase that dratted word from my vocabulary. It was like a woodpecker hammering against my skull. I didn't want another death in my life. But here we were.

"Did she leave the hospital alone?" I asked.

"From what we can tell. She got into the car alone. Prior to that, there were no phone calls to the room or to her cell. No visitors other than Crystal Applegate, Yvette Rodriquez, her sister Mary Lou Pepper, and her kids, Bobby and Madison. And you."

It sounded like he'd thrown in those last two words intentionally. Like they meant something. Like I'd visited her at the hospital, convinced her to leave, then invaded her home and triggered another heart attack. "She asked to see me," I said, already on the defensive.

"So I hear."

"Who'd you hear that from?" I asked, any trace of sleepiness gone. The slats on the window shutters suddenly cracked open, letting in slivers of light. I silently thanked Meemaw.

"Mary Lou. The daughter called 911 first, then she called her aunt."

"And her brother?" I asked.

"He's here at the station, too. The girl's hysterical. The boy's in shock."

"What about their father?"

"He wasn't around—"

"Yes, he was. He was at the hospital."

A beat of silence hung between us before Gavin responded to my statement that Bennett Macaw had been at the hospital. "Interesting."

It was.

"As of now, she died of natural causes."

"What do you mean, right now?" I said hoarsely.

"The fact that she up and left the hospital isn't sittin' right with me," Gavin said. "Until I know why she went home, well, I'm just keepin' an open mind."

That was far from comforting, but I had that same unsettled feeling.

After hanging up with Gavin, I sat on the edge of my bed, stunned. Why hadn't Mary Lou, Madison, nor Bobby mentioned the fact that Bennett Macaw had been in the hospital? I didn't know the man, but I already knew I didn't like him much. The way he'd lit into Mary Lou was a huge red flag. Of course, she'd lit into him, too, so... The fact that he hadn't immediately comforted his kids was another red flag. I thought about how Will would have interacted with Gracie under similar circumstances. He would have wrapped her up in his arms, first, letting his strength seep into her. Then he would have held her by the shoulders and reassured her that she could handle anything.

Bennett Macaw hadn't done any of those things. Those were passing thoughts, though. Front and center was that Sue Ellen was dead. And stranger than that was the fact that she'd left the hospital, apparently of her own accord, only to die at home. But the biggest question of all was whether or not the death had, in fact, been of natural causes.

Chapter Five

Thelma Louise, the grand dame of Nana's herd of goats, pressed her nose against the window of my atelier, staring at me with her otherworldly eyes. Nana had kicked off her Crocs and now stood in the kitchen in her white socks. How she managed to keep them white despite her work on her goat farm was a mystery. It was another of her charms. Mama stood right beside her. She didn't take off her boots and because of that, she'd left a light track of dirt in her wake.

"Not again, Ladybug," Nana said.

I sighed and pushed my glasses back into place from where they'd slipped. "Yes, again. Also, I think Loretta Mae made a horrible mistake in bringing me back to Bliss."

Mama gasped. "What in the world are you talkin' about, darlin'?"

What I was talking about was death. It had knocked on my little farmhouse door too many times since I'd been back in Bliss. Not just death, but murder, and somehow I'd ended up involved in each of them. "Do you think one of my charms is... dark?"

Now Nana gaped at me. "What in tarnation are you goin' on about, Harlow Jane?"

This wasn't the first time I'd wondered if Butch's wish in an Argentinian fountain had bestowed me with a dark charm that brought about people's deaths. I'd realized recently that when each person in my life had died, I hadn't been able to see a special garment for them. It was like the magic inside me knew they'd be gone. A chill slithered through me when I thought about the fact that I could never summon up any clothing for Gavin. All I could ever see him in was his beige law enforcement clothes. I hoped, for Orphie's sake, that I was wrong about this little twist to my ability.

The other thing I'd considered was that one of my charms was actually crime-solving. Given that my oldest ancestor, aka Butch Cassidy, had been one of the most well-known outlaws in American history, that would be an ironic twist of fate.

Either way, here I was, tears welling, thinking about the death of someone else I knew. I slipped into the memory... God, was that just yesterday? Sue Ellen had simply dropped to the pavement in the middle of a raucous conversation with her friends, then died later in her home. Life was far too fragile.

"Darlin'. Harlow!"

Nana snapped her fingers in front of my face and I blinked, coming back to the present. "Sorry, what?"

"Come on, now. What's happening in that mind of yours?"

"Such a terrible loss. It could have happened to any of us."

"No!" Nana and I both jumped at the voice behind us. Mary Lou Pepper stood there, her face tear-stained, the tip of her nose as red as one of Loretta Mae's buttons. "My sister didn't die from a heart attack." Her voice lowered to a harsh whisper. "Someone killed her."

I gaped at her. "But the deputy said—"

"He's wrong."

Behind her, the front door suddenly slammed shut. We all spun around, staring. Mary Lou lurched back. "What the hell—?"

Oh, I knew exactly *what the hell...*

Meemaw.

There wasn't a single trace of a breeze, which forced me to explain away the fact that a gust of wind inside a still house had blown the door closed. Egads, but Loretta Mae had the worst timing. I searched the room, hoping the air wouldn't start to ripple and her shape wouldn't start to form in front of Mary Lou.

"Old house," Nana said from beside me. "It has a mind of its own."

Mama muttered something under her breath. It wasn't hard for me to imagine what she'd said. Something along the lines of, *Dagnabbit, Meemaw, now is not the time.*

I led Mary Lou to the red velvet settee in the front room, which I'd turned into a showroom. Meemaw's old armoire was against one wall. Inside, it was stacked with fabric. In a previous life, the coffee table had been the door of an old house. Now it held my lookbooks and neat stacks of fashion magazines. A rack filled with Prêt-à-Porter clothing I'd made was against another wall. Bliss was a small Texas town and didn't have enough people to sustain a custom dressmaking business so I'd had to get creative. My website was nearly finished and my ready-to-wear collection had become a more affordable option for people who wanted to be, in the words of Heidi Klum, fashion-forward. Zinnia James, wife to Senator Jedediah James, who happened to be a descendant of Etta James—but that was another story for another day—was fashion-forward *and* had become one of my biggest fans and benefactors. Truth be told, the doors of Buttons & Bows were still open in great part due to the various designs I had done for her—including one to help her get back to herself after she'd been a person of interest in the death of the local golf pro.

Life in Bliss was often a tangled web.

I knelt down in front of Mary Lou who had simmered down after her outburst. "I'm so sorry for your loss," I said gently.

She swiped away a rogue tear. "I can't believe she's really gone. I keep thinking she's gonna walk through my door like she always did." She looked up at me, her red-rimmed eyes big and swollen. "Why did she leave the hospital?"

To my mind, that was the most important question. If she hadn't left, would she still be alive? The monitors and nurses would have caught a second heart attack. "You don't have any theories about that?" I asked.

Mary Lou swiped at a rogue tear. "I wish I did."

"She didn't look capable of leaving when I saw her," I said.

Mama sidled up and perched on the edge of the coffee table. "What did the authorities say, sugar?"

Mary Lou's eyes turned hard and frustration etched into her face as she looked first at me, then at Mama. "Nothing. They are saying absolutely nothing other than that it was heart failure. But it wasn't!"

"I'm sure they're looking for clues at the sce—" I'd started to say at the scene of the crime out of habit, but so far there was no crime. I amended it to, "at the house."

Mary Lou gawped at me and her eyes filled again. "Harlow."

I squeezed her hand and lifted my brows, waiting to hear what she was going to say.

"It is a crime scene. My sister was murdered."

Those words swam around in my head, all topsy-turvy,

and I felt dizzy. Another murder in Bliss...and of someone I knew...had me more than a little shaken. Once again I looked at Mama and Nana, my silent question hanging in the air between us. Had Butch Cassidy given me a dark charm when he'd tossed a coin into that magical Argentinian fountain? Had I inadvertently caused Sue Ellen Macaw's death?

Chapter Six

Crystal Applegate and Yvette Rodriquez blew into Buttons & Bows as if they'd been carried straight on the wind of a Texas tornado. They'd never stepped foot in my shop before. Yvette stopped for the briefest second to get her bearings, but the second Crystal saw Mary Lou on the settee she surged toward her. "We got your message! Oh my God, I can't believe it! Mary Lou! Is Sue Ellen...is she really...gone?"

Mary Lou directed her distressed gaze at Crystal. "Murdered," she said bluntly. "She was murdered. And Harlow here is gonna figure out who killed her."

A cacophonous clanking rang out from the innards of the house. Or maybe it was in my head. I jumped up, instantly dizzy and wobbly on my feet. I stumbled backward and right into Mama's bolstering hand. Mary Lou hadn't said anything about wanting me to get involved in solving her sister's supposed murder. "W-w-what?"

"She has a knack for it. You have a knack for it," Mary Lou said to me. "Sue Ellen even said so. She'd *want* you to find out who did this."

That sounded suspiciously like a guilt trip.

Mary Lou spread one hand and tapped the fingers as she ticked off my crime-solving successes. "The golf guy. That man who played Santa Claus. The bead shop girl. That guy with the two—"

"Stop!" I hollered, stomping my booted foot for good measure.

The three friends spun their heads to stare at me. Nana scurried to my side, and Mama stood and pressed her hand to my back to steady me. "It's all true," Yvette said. "I read about all those in the newspaper. Sue Ellen did talk about it. A lot, actually."

Mary Lou dipped her chin and looked at me, then at Mama and Nana, with her glassy eyes. "People say all you Cassidy women are blessed with good fortune. I think solving murders must be one of the things you're especially good at."

So many things about what she'd just said alighted the nerves in my body. The Cassidy women had tried for decades to keep our charms under the radar. During the last year, I'd realized we hadn't been as successful at that as I'd imagined. Not many people spoke about it quite as openly as Mary Lou was currently doing, though. "It's just luck," I said, qualifying that statement in my mind. It was bad luck for the people who'd died, and good luck that I'd had some part in bringing their killers to justice. Either way, luck didn't elevate me to Bliss's premier crime-solver.

"That's not what I've heard," Mary Lou said. She pointed at Mama. "You with the plants. You have some connection to them, right? And you—" She looked at Nana and waved her hand around— "with the goats? I don't even *like* goat cheese, but my God that stuff is like crack."

Despite the terrible circumstance that had brought about that particular compliment, Nana's chest puffed up. She smiled slightly and nodded in agreement, and I actually had to admit that Mary Lou was right. Nana's goat cheese was in a league of its own.

Mary Lou looked at me again, spreading her arms wide to encompass the entire room and the atelier beyond. Her voice had lost its hysterical edge. "And you with your fashion design and sewing? Why do you think we signed up for the class with you? We wanted some of that to rub off on us. And now, instead, Sue Ellen is dead."

"The sheriff will get to the truth," I said. I pressed my hand against my chest. "I'm a fashion designer. *He's* the one who solves crimes."

Crystal patted the air in front of Mary Lou to calm her down. Although from where I stood, she now seemed pretty calm. Overly so, in fact.

"Sweetheart," Crystal said. "Harlow's right. The sheriff'll do his job. If she really was murdered, they'll catch whoever did this."

"My sister *was* murdered," Mary Lou said bluntly, and then she repeated, "Murdered. Listen." Mary Lou's lower lip began to quiver, her steely façade wavering. "Someone had been sending her letters. Warnings."

And just like that, it felt like the first shoe dropped. A high-heeled expensive shoe. A Christian Louboutin. "Warnings about what?" I asked.

Mary Lou swiped at another tear. "I don't know. I don't know! She wouldn't tell me."

Crystal stared. "Do you mean...*threatening letters?* You never told me that!"

Mary Lou gave a defeated shrug. "She didn't take them seriously. You know how she was. She didn't want to raise a ruckus over nothing. But...now I don't think they were nothing."

I stood there, stunned, processing what Mary Lou had said. "So you think someone made it *look* like a heart attack—"

"Exactly."

And just like that, the other red-soled shoe dropped. I found my voice. "And Sue Ellen might have known she was in danger. Where are the letters now?"

"She threw the damn things away."

Crystal sank onto the settee next to Mary Lou and pressed a palm to her forehead. "Oh no, no, no. Did she really?"

Mary Lou nodded. "She said she thought they were empty threats."

"Empty threats about what, though?" Mama asked, her curiosity piqued, too.

Mary Lou threw up her hands helplessly. "I wish I knew. God, how I wish I knew."

"So you never saw any of them?" I asked because I couldn't help myself. Maybe Mary Lou was right. Maybe crime-solving *was* one of my charms.

Mary Lou leaned back and closed her eyes. "She showed me one of them. At the very beginning. It was about a month ago. I wanted her to take it to the police, but she...even then, she didn't want to."

"What'd it say?" Mama asked, and we all nodded to say we wanted to know that, too.

"It was so ridiculous."

Clearly not if the person who'd sent them had killed her, I thought.

"What do you mean, honey?" Crystal asked.

"It was like one of those ransom notes you see in the movies with the letters and words cut from magazines. It said: *I know what happened.*"

The stack of magazines I had on my coffee table suddenly toppled over as if another gust of wind had blown through the house. The one on top flopped open and the pages inside fluttered. Meemaw again. I shifted, closing the space between Mama, Nana, and me to block Meemaw's shenanigans from view. Was there something Loretta Mae wanted to communicate through her primitive hunt-and-peck game? If so, it had to wait.

Nana folded one arm across her chest, cocking the other at the elbow and stroking her chin. "Why would anyone be threatening her?"

Another excellent question. Sue Ellen had come across as just a normal Bliss woman with nothing out of the ordinary going on in her life. Based on what Mary Lou was saying, there might well have been some skeleton in her closet. Once again, all of our gazes swung to the dead woman's sister. Mary Lou seemed to feel the weight of our stares. Her eyes flew open and she pulled her head back like a turtle yanking its head back into its shell. Only Mary Lou's head had nowhere to go. "I have no idea. Truly, I don't. If I did, I'd have told that deputy or the sheriff. If I did, I would have helped Sue Ellen get out of whatever trouble she got herself into." She looked up at me with pleading eyes. "Harlow, please, please, please. You have to help me. I need to know who did this."

When I looked at her, my heart broke. I didn't have a sister, but I had my brother Red. And I had Mama and Nana. And Orphie and Josie and Madelyn. And Will and Gracie. If anything ever happened to *any* of them, I wouldn't rest until I had answers. I wouldn't leave a single stone unturned. I couldn't sit back and do nothing knowing the anguish Mary Lou was in. "Of course I will," I said. "I'll do everything I can to help."

Chapter Seven

Doing everything I could to help meant calling up the local authorities and filling them in about the threatening letters Sue Ellen Macaw had received. I told Mary Lou she should do it, but she begged me to make the call. So I did. Not thirty minutes later, Deputy Gavin McClaine sauntered into Buttons & Bows like he owned the place, gripping the handles of a reusable grocery bag. His dad marrying my mom had made him my stepbrother, but it hadn't made us friends.

"Harlow," he said dryly.

"Gavin," I replied.

He frowned at me and I knew it was because I'd dropped the formality of using his title. I wasn't about to stand on formalities in the privacy of my shop, even though I knew the omission grated on him.

He set the bag down and withdrew a narrow notepad and pen from his uniform's shirt pocket. Beige, beige, beige. I'd yet to see the man in anything other than beige.

He skipped the small talk. "Tell me about the threatening notes," he said, pen poised over his notepad.

"I can't tell you much. Mary Lou—Sue Ellen's sister—"

"I know the names of the key players in this drama," he said.

His attitude grated on me, but I let it go. It wouldn't do me a lick of good to rile him up. "Okay. Well, Mary Lou told me this morning that Sue Ellen had been receiving threatening letters, which I told you. She said she saw one of them, but Sue Ellen threw them all away. She didn't take them seriously, apparently. Mary Lou also said she doesn't know what they were about."

"And why are *you* the one telling me this? I questioned Ms. Pepper yesterday. She didn't mention any of this."

"I think she had some time to think about it. But now she's adamant that Sue Ellen's death wasn't natural *or* accidental."

His eyes snapped to mine at this. "Is that right? Does she have any ideas on who might have wanted her sister dead? And how they caused Sue Ellen to have another heart attack?"

I answered the questions in order. "Yes, that's right. No, I don't think she has any ideas. And I have no clue."

"And she wanted you, intrepid crime-solver that you are, to help me solve the case, is that it?"

I adjusted my glasses and looked at him with a forced smile. "Such a big vocabulary word, Gavin."

"Guess all that schoolin' paid off," he said dryly, not missing a beat. "I'll be contactin' Ms. Pepper about this. If you hear from her, you can go ahead and let her know that."

I doubt I'd see her before he tracked her down so I didn't respond to that. Instead, I nodded at the bag he'd set down. "What's that?"

He slipped his notepad and pen back into his shirt pocket and bent to pick up the bag. "A gift from beyond the grave."

As if in response to his words, the door slammed shut behind him even though, once again, not even the ghost of a breeze stirred the air inside or outside. I sighed. This particular parlor trick of Meemaw's was getting old.

Gavin spun his head to look at the door and his frown deepened. He didn't know about Meemaw or the fact that the Cassidy women didn't pass straight to the afterworld, but instead became ghosts. Loretta Mae was an eternal presence in my little farmhouse. I was pretty sure that even Cressida, her mother, flitted around, usually in the corporeal form of a ladybug. But my stepbrother was none the wiser about any of it... or so I hoped.

"Beyond the grave?" I repeated as my gaze zeroed in on the tote.

"Found this in Sue Ellen Macaw's house. Apparently, it's for you."

He held the bag out. Our fingers brushed as I took it from him and I readied myself for a flash of Gavin dressed in something other than his deputy's uniform. Dang. Nothing. It frustrated me...but more than that, it concerned me. I came back to yet another question that had started to take solid root in my mind: Could I foretell a person's death? If I wasn't able to summon up an image of them in a custom-made garment, did that mean they wouldn't be around long enough for me to make it for them?

I shook my head to clear away the thought. I wouldn't let those roots spread. I couldn't. There was no accounting for taste, but Orphie was falling in love with Gavin. Obviously, I wanted him to live.

Plus, the Cassidy women had single charms, not multiple charms, right? Butch's wish couldn't have bestowed me with the ability to sew hopes and dreams into a garment, bring about death through a lack of vision, *and* solve crimes, could it? The first was my charm. The other two were mere coincidences. I hoped.

I looked inside. Sitting right on top was a bent index card

with my name and a partial message hurriedly scrawled across it in black Sharpie:

Harlow. It's got to come out. Ch—

The last letters turned into a scribble as if she dropped the pen. Or was interrupted.

Gavin rocked back on his booted heels and waited while I pulled a pink tissue-wrapped bundle from the bag. Neatly folded inside the thin paper was a white garment, yellowed with age. I unfolded it and shook it out. It was a lightweight sleeveless dress with a dropped waist and ballerina-style bodice, cap sleeves, and a full skirt. A dusting of sequins spread across the shoulders on the bodice. A net petticoat floated under the skirt and a metal zipper closed the back. I felt the fabric of the skirt in my hands. Silk.

The dress was very reminiscent of Christian Dior from the 1950s. Surely it wasn't *actually* one of the famed designer's dresses. But when I looked at the label sewn onto the fabric next to the zipper closure, I knew it was. The rectangular strip of subtly striped fabric was embroidered with two words: Neiman Marcus.

"Holy moly," I said.

Gavin's eye twitched as he looked at me. "What?"

I held the dress out. "This is a vintage Christian Dior."

"Is that supposed to mean something to me?"

I gaped. This guy would be a disaster at Trivial Pursuit. "Christian Dior? The designer? Surely you've heard of him?"

He shrugged.

"Sue Ellen had an original Christian Dior from Neiman Marcus," I said as if that was enough to explain my awe. From his blank expression, it clearly wasn't. "For a country girl from Bliss, Texas, that's big, Gavin. Really big."

"So she just went to Neiman Marcus in Dallas and bought it. So what?"

"No, no, no. It's from the 1950s. Sue Ellen wasn't even born when this dress was made. She couldn't have bought it herself."

"So it belonged to her mother, or she got it secondhand. What's the big deal?"

I showed him the faint lines drawn onto the skirt of the dress with fabric chalk. "She drew on it. On a vintage Dior." Why would she have done that? I spread out the skirt as I looked at the markings. They delineated delicate branches with lacy leaves and a profusion of daisies moving upward from the hem, stretching toward the bodice. A few of the stems had been painted green. So Sue Ellen had mapped out a lovely design to customize the dress and she'd started painting it herself.

I didn't know how much the garment would have been worth if it was in pristine condition. As it was now, yellowed with age and the beginnings of a flower garden painted on it, the value was probably nil. Which meant it had been sentimental for Sue Ellen. Maybe Gavin was right. Maybe it *had* belonged to her mother.

Gavin peered at the chalk lines. "Why'd she draw on it?"

"So she could paint it," I said. I fanned out the skirt and showed him the bits she'd already done.

He snapped his fingers. "Right. That fabric painting class. Why in the world someone would take the time to paint flowers on a dress is beyond me."

"You better not let Orphie hear you say that. It happens to be one of her specialties."

He frowned at that and issued a bewildered, "Hmph." On the one hand, he was very into Orphie. On the other hand, he didn't really get what her life's passion was. I wasn't sure their relationship had a future if he didn't at least try to understand. He blinked, chasing away whatever discordant thoughts had been bouncing around in his head, and nodded at the dress I held. "So the note...she wanted to make sure you got that out? The chalk?"

"I guess," I said. It would have to be dry-cleaned for that to happen.

"So what'd'ya think? She wanted you to finish painting it?"

"I guess?" I said again, this time heavy with uncertainty. How...and when...had she put this dress in this bag and written my name on the card? What was it about this dress that was so important to Sue Ellen? Another question came quickly on the heels of those. We'd all been wondering why Sue Ellen had left the hospital that night. I looked at the garment I held. What if this was why she'd gone home? Was this what she'd wanted to talk to me about?

I headed for my atelier with Gavin following behind me. As I slipped the dress onto one of my three dress forms, I shook away the feeling that Sue Ellen had known something bad was coming. If she hadn't, she would have finished the dress herself. But she had left the hospital, presumably putting the dress into the bag with my name on the notecard to make sure I got it. It was as if she'd known she wasn't going to live through the night. A tremble crawled up my spine. Sue Ellen *knew* someone was trying to kill her. And if that was the case, why would making sure I got this dress be one of her priorities? It couldn't be about the value of a Dior since, technically, it had been defaced.

I couldn't answer any of the questions spinning through my mind so I answered Gavin's instead. "If Sue Ellen wanted me to finish it for her, that's what I'm going to do."

The thing was, she was already dead, so my charm

couldn't make her hopes and dreams come true, but maybe painting what she'd drawn would help me connect with her somehow....or figure out who killed her. That, at least, was my hope.

Gavin shook his head as he headed to the door. "Death sure does seem to follow you around, Harlow. Maybe you should put a warning sign on your door. *Clients Beware*."

I lowered my glasses to the tip of my nose and peered at him from above the frames. "Nice, Gavin," I said. He stepped out onto the porch and before either he or I could shut the door, it slammed close with a hearty bang.

"Thanks, Meemaw," I said, but I frowned at the way he'd put into words my very thoughts from earlier. What had Butch Cassidy done?

Chapter Eight

I am nothing if not a perfectionist. Before I really dug into painting Sue Ellen's vintage dress, I wanted to see the flowers that had inspired her. That meant taking a drive out to the house where she and Mary Lou had grown up. Mary Lou didn't answer her cell when I called, so I tried Crystal—also no answer—then Yvette. "It's out on FM 3170," she said when I asked her for the address. "There's an iron gate and two pillars. It says Four Peppers Ranch across the top. You can't miss it. If you get to the railroad tracks, you've gone too far. " She paused for a second then said, "I can go with you."

I welcomed the company. Maybe Yvette could offer up something more about Sue Ellen and the mysterious threatening letters. Sometimes, I'd come to realize, people didn't know what they knew. I checked on Earl Gray, making sure the little teacup pig had water, then climbed into Buttercup and rumbled across town to pick up Yvette. When I'd first met her, I'd thought that she could use a bit of a makeover. Now, in the wake of losing one of her closest friends, there was no doubt. She'd pulled her hair back into a floppy ponytail, her skin looked pallid, as if it had lost three shades of olive since the death, and her clothes were wrinkled and hung loose on her frame. It had only been a few days, but it looked as if she'd lost ten pounds.

"Are you eating?" I asked her, worried by how thin she looked.

"I don't have much of an appetite," she answered. She seemed to register my look of concern and quickly added, "But I'm fine."

She turned to look out the passenger window. She didn't seem to want to talk and for a while, we bounced along the Farm to Market road in silence. Finally, I couldn't stand it anymore. "Yvette, what do you think about what Mary Lou said? You didn't know about the letters Sue Ellen was getting?"

She didn't budge. Didn't move a muscle, and for a few seconds I thought she hadn't heard me. I inhaled and started to ask again when she turned. "I knew. She told me about them after she got the second one, but Mary Lou's right. She didn't seem concerned about them. I never saw one, though."

The memory of Sue Ellen's former husband on the outskirts of the hospital waiting room surfaced. "What about her ex?"

"Bennett? No love lost between him and Mary Lou, but that wasn't his fault." She shrugged. "I think he's all right, though. I was sorry when they split up."

"What's the story there?"

Yvette shook her head. "Sisters. You know how it is. I think Mary Lou was always a little jealous. She never got married. Her one true love, as she likes to put it, up and dumped her, but Sue Ellen had a boyfriend in high school. Christopher. He was a looker." Her eyelids fluttered and she looked up, apparently remembering just how much of a looker he was. "Sue Ellen was crazy about him. We all thought he was crazy about her, too. He even gave her a promise ring. When they broke up, Sue Ellen was a mess. That's when her mom got her into gardening. A distraction, you know? All Sue Ellen did was plant flowers and then sit and watch them grow. Eventually, she found Bennett. Mary Lou was just bitter, I think. Sue Ellen had *two* guys who'd loved her and she had none. In the end, though, she took it out on Bennett."

I glanced at her. "Relationships are complicated," I said. I'd seen it over and over. Whether it was between sisters or siblings or parents or friends, there were always ups and downs. And too often I'd seen people go off the rails because of those complications.

"Mary Lou wanted to be in love," Yvette continued. "But she loved Sue Ellen. When Christopher dumped Sue Ellen, and then when Sue Ellen and Bennett got divorced, Mary Lou went into pure protection mode. It's that sister connection, you know? It's like, she could say or feel whatever she wanted about her sister, but no one else could, right? That was always Mary Lou."

It made sense to me. They had a history together as sisters, just like my brother and I did. We knew things about each other that no one else did. And we'd always, *always* have each other.

As Yvette and I slipped back into silence, I thought about the Pepper sisters. I felt bad for Mary Lou that she'd needed to tie her happiness to the idea of having a man in her life. One thing I realized when I left home to try my luck at fashion design in New York was that I had to make my own happiness. If I didn't, then what did I have to offer to someone else? Coming back home to Bliss had been orchestrated by Meemaw—after all, she got whatever she wanted—but *I'd* created Buttons & Bows; *I'd* rebuilt friendships with old friends and formed new ones; *I'd* come to love Gracie, easily slipping into a pseudo sister/aunt role with her, and it was one of my most cherished relationships, and *I'd* realized that I didn't need New York City or to work for the mega-successful Maximillian in order to be happy. Since coming back home to Bliss, I'd learned who I was and what I wanted.

We had to be happy by ourselves before we could be happy with someone else. I firmly believed that. When I'd fallen head over heels for Will Flores, it was not because Loretta Mae had wanted it to be. It was not because I needed a man in my life. It was because we fit. We complemented each other, but we weren't dependent on each other. Will Flores, more than anyone (besides Mama, Nana, and Meemaw, of course), believed in me, and I believed in him. Together we were a good team.

The same was true for Nana and Dalton Massie, my Granddaddy, and for Mama and Hoss McClaine. I wanted every woman to have that kind of love.

Yvettee's voice broke into my thoughts. "It's coming up," she said, pointing out the window to the right. I slowed Buttercup and rumbled up to a gate just like Yvette had described on the phone. Two stone pillars sat on either side of the drive. Wooden fencing ran out from either side, encircling the ranch. The front wrought iron gate was closed, and just like Yvette had said, Four Peppers Ranch was written in block letters and created an archway at the entrance. Four iron horses marched across the top. The first one, in the lead, had a cowboy mounted on it, while the other three had cowgirls, delineated by long braids. Yvette followed my gaze. "They're for Mary Lou and Sue Ellen's daddy, mama, and the two of them. Four Peppers."

"Do they still live here?" I asked. "Their parents, I mean."

"No. Mr. Pepper passed about ten years ago," Yvette said. "Mrs. Pepper died a few months ago."

I noticed the For Sale sign sitting off to the left of the ranch entrance, a shrub hiding it. "They're selling?"

Yvette squinted her eyes, registered the sign, then sat up

straight. "Oh. I didn't know they listed it. Sue Ellen never wanted to sell. I guess Mary Lou finally talked her into it."

I let that thought spool around my mind for a few seconds and it unsettled me. Finally, my unease settled in the pit of my stomach like a rock because if Sue Ellen never wanted to sell and Mary Lou did, that could be the makings of a motive. The fact was, I'd seen people murdered for far less.

Chapter Nine

Yvette filled me in on the background of Four Peppers Ranch. Clive Pepper had raised cattle for as long as she could remember. "Betsy—that's Sue Ellen and Mary Lou's mother—she sold them off after her husband died," Yvette said. "Eventually Mary Lou had wanted to sell. She wanted Betsy to move in with Sue Ellen. Sue Ellen and Bennett were already getting divorced by then, and Mary Lou thought it would help them both."

"She could have moved in with Mary Lou, though, right? Did it have to be Sue Ellen?" I asked.

"Mary Lou was a daddy's girl. Sue Ellen was tight with their mama, so it made more sense—at least to Mary Lou—for Betsy to stay with Sue Ellen."

I sensed a but. Right on cue, Yvette said, "But Sue Ellen still had her kids at home. She was adjusting to the breakup with Bennett. She didn't want to disrupt Madison's and Bobby's lives with another change. In the end, Betsy just stayed put. Honestly, I don't think she ever wanted to leave in the first place." She cupped her hand over her eyes and looked at the For Sale sign again.

Something didn't smell right. A conversation from the fabric painting class at the Arts Center came back to me. The four women had been talking about the Carrie Underwood song, "Black Cadillac". Sue Ellen had pivoted and said that they could bury her under the daisies. She'd said, with no ifs, ands, or buts, that she wasn't selling the old house. That she didn't want some new people destroying the things she'd created. I brought this up to Yvette. "What do you think?"

She thought for a moment then said, "That's how Sue Ellen's always felt..."

"That she didn't want to sell?"

"Right."

We both looked at the For Sale sign. If that was the case, Mary Lou hadn't wasted any time in listing the place.

Yvette rattled off four numbers, which I punched into the keypad on the left side of the entrance. "The code's been the same for as long as I've known them," she said.

That probably made things much easier for deliveries when it was a working ranch. Changing the gate passcode wasn't as critical as constantly changing your online passwords. The gate opened, bouncing to a stop. After I drove Buttercup through, the sensor activated and it launched back into action, closing behind me. In order to leave the property, I'd have to wait for the gate to open again. There could be no fast getaway here, I thought in passing.

I'd expected a bumpy ride on a dirt drive, but the road to the ranch was black asphalt. I cruised along at a low speed so I could take it all in. Pecan trees on either side of the road stood like soldiers. Flat acres of grass spread into the distance on either side. At some point in the ranch's history, cattle had probably grazed the land, but now it was green and velvety from massive amounts of irrigation and late summer rain. "It's gorgeous," I said.

"Mmm," Yvette said in agreement. "I used to love coming

out here. All the kids would pile into the back of Mr. Pepper's pickup truck and he'd drive us through the cattle. A bull chased us one time and, oh my stars, I really thought it was going to catch us." She laughed at the memory. I had similar antics from my teenage years with my granddaddy, others on my own or with friends, wreaking havoc in a small Texas town when there was nothin' else to do. I'd landed in Hoss McClaine's office on far too many occasions.

I smiled. Good times.

When I saw the house, I saw that once again my expectations were way off. Once I'd seen the asphalt road, I'd expected a sprawling expensive house. Instead, I was greeted by a modest ranch-style home that was well-kept but much smaller than a ranch of this magnitude deserved. "I haven't been inside for years, but I bet it needs a lot of updating. I bet whoever buys it will do a tear-down," Yvette said sadly.

"You're probably right," I said. Either that or a complete gut job and massive remodel. I didn't even want to think about the price tag for the ranch, let alone a remodel or a new build. The road gave to a circular driveway in front of the house. I parked in the shade under a cluster of trees.

"What are you looking for?" Yvette asked.

We'd been so busy with other conversations that I hadn't told her. "Sue Ellen left a dress for me to finish. She drew flowers onto it and started to paint it, but before I start, I wanted to see them in person. I mean, a daisy is a daisy, but...I don't know...it doesn't feel right to paint just any daisies. I want *her* daisies. The ones she loved so much."

Flowerbeds ran along the front of the house, summer blooms brightening the landscape. But there wasn't a single daisy in sight. Yvette started walking. "They're in the back. This way."

We walked to the end of the east side of the house. As we

turned, a massive red barn and stables appeared. A corral and arena were beyond that. "They had horses, too?"

"Oh yeah. Betsy gave us all lessons in the summers when we were little. That was the best. So fun."

"It sounds like you have so many great memories here," I said. It was exactly how I felt about my farmhouse. Meemaw had taught me to sew there. Nana's goats had always been a fixture. It was the gathering place for the Cassidy family and had been ever since Cressida Cassidy built it. Unless I had no other choice, I would never let it go. If I was to believe Yvette, Mary Lou was willing to let this place go easily, which made me sad.

"So many memories," Yvette said wistfully. "I missed those horses when they were gone."

"What happened to them?" I asked.

"Mary Lou never took to 'em much. She could ride but she never loved it like Sue Ellen. Sue Ellen and Christopher used to go on trail rides, but after they broke up, Sue Ellen wouldn't even look at a horse anymore. Since Mary Lou didn't like 'em, their daddy up and sold 'em all."

We turned again at the back of the house where an aggregate cement patio spread out from a sliding glass door. Pots sat in clusters at the corners and an enclosed vegetable garden without any plants was on the other side. A separate bed away from the house exploded with daisies. It was as if seeds had been tossed without any rhyme or reason, the flowers bursting forth from where they'd landed. A cement bench sat off to one side on a flattened area. I could see why Sue Ellen loved the flowers so much. Yvette sighed reminiscently. "If I close my eyes I can see Sue Ellen sitting on that bench, surrounded by her daisies," she said.

"They *are* beautiful." As I walked closer to get a better look and to snap some pictures with my phone, a man's voice drifted across the expanse of the yard. I turned and saw the corner of a big, black 4x4 parked behind the barn. I couldn't see anyone, but I could clearly make out the guy's voice as he carried on a conversation with someone. "Yvette," I said with a hiss. "Someone's here."

Yvette hurried to my side and followed my line of vision. "The realtor, maybe? Showing the—"

She broke off, staring. "What is it?" I asked.

"That's Bennett Macaw's truck."

Now *I* stared. And listened. The last time I'd seen Sue Ellen's ex, it had been an out-and-out duel with Mary Lou. Raised voices and enough anger to power up a generator during a North Texas ice storm. Now, though, his voice was calm, and whoever he was speaking with—on the phone, I realized—wasn't raising his ire as much as his former sister-in-law had. Bits of his side of the conversation carried over to where we stood. "It's impossible. She would have told me," he snapped, then, after a moment of silence when he was presumably listening, he said, "It's just not possible. There's nothing here. You're way off base."

Who was he talking to, and why was he here at his ex-wife's family's ranch? I started to march to the barn to get the answer straight from the horse's mouth, but Yvette grabbed my sleeve and yanked me back. "Let's go," she said.

I resisted. "No, let's talk to him."

"No," Yvette said. "We shouldn't be here without permission."

She was right, but neither should Bennett Macaw. Confronting him, though, probably wouldn't do a lick of good. I weighed my options and decided I would find a better way to talk to him, so I let Yvette drag me back to Buttercup. Before long, we'd left the ranch behind.

The whole way home, I wondered what in tarnation

Bennett Macaw was doing on the property of his deceased ex-wife's family, and who he was talking to. Who would have told him what? What wasn't there? And who was off base? Things were getting curiouser and curiouser.

Chapter Ten

I took a chance and called Mary Lou after I dropped Yvette back home. She'd wanted me to help get to the truth behind her sister's death, which is what I felt compelled to do now more than ever. The value of the family property going straight to her was a pretty good motive, but surely she wouldn't have asked for my help if she was guilty.

Unless she was also diabolical.

For the moment, I was going to choose not to believe that. That led me to Bennett Macaw. I wanted to talk to him, but I didn't want to throw anyone under the proverbial bus—not without proof. I spun a tale, telling her that he'd dropped something in the hospital the other night and I wanted to return it to him.

"I can do it," she said, but only half-heartedly.

"Oh no! It's no trouble."

She didn't need convincing. "He used to go to Villa Farina on the square every morning for an Italian pastry and a cup of coffee. 6:25 on the dot. He probably still does," she said as if his commitment to his routine irritated her. For me, that commitment would come in handy. Just the idea of waking up that early made me yawn, but I was determined. Whatever sibling rivalry had existed in Mary Lou's relationship with her sister, she wanted answers. I did, too. I still kept the fact that she'd already listed the house in the back of my mind, but for now I wasn't going to focus on it.

I decided casually bumping into Bennett Macaw at Villa Farina was the best idea. I set my alarm for 5:45 AM, which was well before me or Nana's roosters ever cracked open an eye. When it rang, I hit snooze three times before waking with a jolt at 6:05. My feet landed on the hardwood floor with a thud and an accidental nudge to Earl Gray's fluffy bed. He snorted from the disturbance in his sleep and then settled back into his slumber.

"So jealous, Earl," I said through a yawn, but I was on a mission so I wiped the sleep away from my eyes and got myself ready. It was too early for fashion and I figured I wouldn't see any prospective clients at this ungodly hour anyway, so I went with an ancient pair of button-fly jeans that had been washed so many times the denim felt like silk, and a lightweight black sweater. I brushed my curls into a high ponytail and glanced in the mirror as I patted down the flyaways. I gently touched the bit of blond hair that sprouted from my temple and looked like an offset skunk's stripe. I leaned over the sink to get a better look. Was it brighter than normal? "Meemaw!"

Earl Gray grunted, but otherwise, it was utterly silent. Not a single pipe clanged. The pages of the books and magazines at my bedside didn't rustle. No otherworldly howls echoed through the halls. My ghostly great-grandmother didn't make a peep when I actually wanted her to.

The roots of my blond stripe tingled. I pressed the pads of my fingertips down on the strands of hair to quiet the sensation. "Meemaw," I said again, this time more to myself than to the house at large. "I need some answers." Those questions about the depth of my charm—or charms—had been weighing on me again. Butch Cassidy had been an outlaw. He wasn't really known for his nice side, his love story with my great-great-great grandmother, Texana, notwithstanding. That romance was a little bit of a mystery, in fact, especially once I'd discovered that he'd been with Etta Place, who was part of his Wild Bunch gang, around the same time as he'd been with Texana, and that that little union had resulted in a different Cassidy line. Good grief, but what a tangled web those outlaws weaved.

The question of whether or not Butch had bestowed on me a dark charm that ran alongside my ability to sew wishes and dreams into clothes kept surfacing. Did I actually bring about death?

A shudder crawled up my spine. I didn't want it to be true. I liked the idea that the garments I made helped people realize their dreams. It was a much nicer bit of magic.

But the fact was, I did seem to have a knack for bringing murderers to justice, and since I hadn't had the opportunity to sew something for Sue Ellen—and I hoped and prayed I didn't have a thing to do with her death—that left trying to solve her murder as the only thing I *could* do—as much for my peace of mind as for justice.

The sun was just beginning its ascent when I stepped onto the porch. By the time I walked from the house to Villa Farina on the town square, the sunrise had colored the sky with a wash of pastel watercolors. More people than I imagined were up and about for the early hour. It made me think that maybe it wasn't so early after all. Inside, Villa Farina was still waking up. The buildings on the square were old and drafty. A chill from the night hung in the air. It would burn off as the day progressed and bodies warmed the space.

A young man with sleepy eyes took orders at the register

while Gina, who had been a staple at the cafe since before I'd moved back to Bliss, was the barista. A black bandana held back her two-toned black and red hair and her teal-colored apron looked freshly laundered. By the time her shift was finished, I imagined it would be stained with flour and coffee, and other stains from the day.

She looked like she came straight from the Jersey shore... until she spoke and her languid Texas drawl came out. "Good*ness*," she said when she caught a glimpse of me, emphasizing the second part of the word. "You're sure up and out early."

I leaned one hip against the bar and watched as she steamed milk in a small stainless steel frothing pitcher. "I am that," I said, stifling a yawn.

She notched her head toward the order line. "Coffee?"

The aroma of roasting coffee beans tickled my senses, but it felt a little too early for my cup of joe. I needed to wake up on my own for a little while before I infused my body with caffeine. "In a little while," I said.

She finished her frothing and flipped the switch to stop the flow of steam. She worked without thinking in the same way I did. She picked up a damp cloth and wiped the steam arm, then she poured the hot milk into a cup of already prepared espresso, slowing at the end to create a design in the froth. She set it down and hollered, "Mark, vanilla latte!"

Mark had been waiting at the napkin station. He sauntered up, took his freshly made latte, and left. Gina had already moved on to the next order, pouring milk, steaming, creating a layer of froth, and pouring it into a cup of espresso.

"I heard about that poor lady who died," she said in a much quieter voice. We'd had more than one chitchat about the death of Macon Vance, which had turned Bliss society (such as it was) on its booted heal. Gina knew my experience with death. She just didn't know that this one might be murder.

"Sue Ellen Pepper-Macaw," I said.

Gina shook her head sadly, but she was a professional and there was no rest for the barista. She picked up the disposable cup, read the order written on the side of it, and set to work brewing a double shot of espresso, pouring oat milk into a clean pitcher. Her expression didn't show recognition. "You didn't know her?" I asked.

She frowned. "Sue Ellen, Sue Ellen, Sue Ellen," she repeated the name as if it might trigger a memory. Instead, she frowned. "The name's not ringing a bell."

Gina worked nearly every morning, so if Sue Ellen had been a morning regular, she would have known the name. I leaned in again, lowering my voice so only she could hear. "Do you know her ex, Bennett Macaw?"

Recognition lit up her eyes. She lifted her gaze to me while she continued steaming. "Oh my God, *that* Macaw? The lawyer? He's a regular. Oh wow, that's awful."

Yvette had said he was a lawyer and once I'd gotten home from our trip to the ranch, I'd looked him up. He handled mineral rights, which was always a big deal in Texas. If you were sitting on the right kind of property, they could be worth a whole lotta money. He wasn't since he and Sue Ellen were divorced, but I had to wonder why he'd been at Four Peppers Ranch. Did he know something Mary Lou didn't? "Right."

She lifted her chin toward the cafe door and a stocky man who strolled in. "He's like clockwork," she said. "Six twenty-five every morning."

His head was angled down and he cradled a cell phone in two hands, his thumbs moving over the screen at a breakneck pace. If texting was a Nascar event, he'd be in the lead, for sure. He looked familiar, but I hadn't gotten a good look at him at the hospital or the ranch. "That's him?" I asked Gina.

"Yep, that's him," she said. "Triple shot caramel macchiato."

She knew people by their drink orders as much as by their names. I was the same, only I recalled the outfits people wore or the ones I'd made for them. "Thanks," I said and I gave her a thumbs up. I left the barista counter and scooted into line right behind Bennett Macaw. I guess I wanted coffee after all.

Chapter Eleven

"Excuse me, sir?"

The man in front of me turned halfway. He was heavyset with weighty jowls pulling his face down. He looked haggard and his red-rimmed eyes and puffy dark bags beneath them told me he hadn't been sleeping well. Grief over losing his ex-wife, or something else? He raised his brows as if to say, *Who, me?*

I smiled. "Are you Bennett Macaw?"

"I am," he said warily.

"The Bennett Macaw from Texas Mineral Brokers?"

He looked me up and down—a little too blatantly for my taste—before settling on my face. He pinched his brows together as if he might recognize me. "Do I know you?"

"Not yet," I said amiably. "I've just...I heard about your firm and looked you up. I'm so glad you have photos on your website," I said, as a way of explaining how I knew who he was. "Calling to schedule a consultation is on my To Do list—but here you are! I moved back to Bliss about a year ago and I inherited my great-grandmother's house—"

"Hello...?" The teenager at the front counter raised his voice. "Can I help you?"

We both turned to look at the young man. Bennett Macaw stepped forward and rattled off his order. Gina had nailed it. Triple shot caramel macchiato. I shot a glance at Gina who lifted one side of her mouth in a satisfied grin.

Macaw paid and stepped over to the barista counter to wait for his drink. I quickly ordered a small brown sugar latte, handed over the five-dollar bill I'd tucked into my pocket before leaving the house—which was barely enough for the fancy coffee—and sidled up next to Macaw as nonchalantly as possible. I didn't want to appear too eager, but I needn't have worried.

Gina handed him his large latte, and immediately handed mine over, too. Bless her, she'd made sure we got our drinks at the same time so he wouldn't leave before I could talk to him. I flashed her a smile, took my drink, and matched Bennett Macaw's stride as he walked out.

"You were saying something about your grandmother's house?" he asked, and I smiled to myself. I'd hooked him with the word *consultation*. I was now a potential client who he could bill. He stopped and turned to me.

"My great-grandmother's," I said. "Actually, it's mine. I inherited it from her after she passed."

"I am sorry for your loss."

Ah if he only knew that she wasn't really gone. "Thank you." I let a moment of silence linger for Meemaw then said, "I've had some inquiries about selling the mineral rights and someone mentioned your company. I just don't know if I should do it. What if they're trying to take advantage of me? How do I know what's a fair price?"

The second the words were out of my mouth his demeanor had changed, shifting from wary to bright-eyed and bushy-tailed. I looked at him as innocently as possible. "Those are very smart questions, Ms..."

"Cassidy," I said. "Harlow Cassidy."

"Well, Ms. Cassidy, it's nice to meet you. Let me tell you something right now. Drilling rights in Texas *are* big business. You did the right thing by wanting to talk to me about it." I'm sure he thought so. More money in his pocket if I hired him to negotiate my nonexistent mineral rights. He fished a business card from his wallet and handed it over. "If you'd give my office a call, tell them we spoke, and we can set up an appointment."

"For today?" I asked, hoping I wasn't coming across as too eager. "These people are relentless. I just don't know what to say to them."

He hesitated, but only for a few seconds. He'd tucked his phone into his jacket pocket, but now he pulled it out again. In a deft one-thumb maneuver, he called up his calendar. "I can probably squeeze you in between appointments this afternoon. How's one-thirty?"

I tapped my chin with my index finger and looked skyward, pretending to consider. "Perfect," I said after a few seconds.

I tucked his business card into my pocket and left him to his coffee and morning and got ready to carry on with mine. I wanted to start painting Sue Ellen's flowers, and the next fabric painting class at the Arts Center was this morning, too. I hurried home. Painting Sue Ellen's dress wasn't the only thing on my fashion plate at the moment. I'd designed three little black dresses—each different—for three different women who were attending the same museum event in Dallas. They were mostly done, but I had to finish the hems and the detail work, which for one of them meant sewing tiny, perfectly spaced, and equal-sized stitches around the scalloped bodice. Tedious and time-consuming, but I was always willing to do whatever needed to be done for the sake of fashion.

A few hours later, my fingers a little stiff from holding the short needle, I headed back to the Arts Center. I hadn't seen Mary Lou or Crystal since they'd converged on Buttons & Bows, and I hadn't seen Yvette since our trip to Four Peppers Ranch. I had no idea if any of them would show up to class but I'd packed up my tote bags, loaded them into Buttercup's passenger seat, and drove across town. I waved to Tawny who sat in her little office behind the glass partition. I stopped to say hello, setting my tote bags down so I could chat for a minute without having my arms feel like they might fall right off. Her usually spiky hair was subdued, laying flat, and brushed back today. It made her look completely different. Less big city, more small town.

"Hey," she said.

"Hey," I said back.

That was it for pleasantries. Tawny cut right to the chase. She leaned toward me, her eyes wide. "I heard Sue Ellen left the hospital and died in her house. What the hell? Why would she do that?"

"I have no idea," I said.

"So she had two heart attacks? If that doesn't want to make you take care of yourself, I don't know what will." She tapped a brown paper back that sat on her desk next to her collection of photos. "An orange, a banana, and healthy granola. I'm turning over a new leaf."

I didn't tell her that Sue Ellen's second heart attack might not have actually been a heart attack. Smothering? That was the only thing I could think of that might be mistaken for a heart attack. That suspicion was on a need-to-know basis, and she didn't need to know. Instead, I said, "Good for you. I need to do that, too." Thanks to Nana and her Sundance Kids, my diet was a little too heavy with dairy.

"I heard the deputy was at her house after it...happened."

"Gavin? Probably normal protocol," I said, impressed with her intel. Apparently, her position as assistant director of the Arts Center made her privy to all kinds of information. Small towns—where everyone knew everything. "Her daughter found her and called 911 so..."

"Gavin," she said with a dreamy sigh. "Such a sexy name."

My brow furrowed. "If you say so."

She nodded with vigor. "Oh, I say so. One hundred percent. And he's such a hottie. Sadly too young for me, but if he doesn't mind, I wouldn't mind."

Younger than her by close to two decades, I thought wryly. That was a few *too* many years apart. I frowned, a little hung up on her description of Gavin McClaine. I guess he *was* considered attractive by some. Orphie had described him in ways I didn't care to think about. I shook away those wayward thoughts and changed the subject. "Gavin brought me one of Sue Ellen's dresses so I can finish painting it."

She'd been doodling on a little notepad as we talked, but now she looked up, brows pinched. "She'd dead, so why finish —" She slapped one hand over her mouth. "Oh my God, I'm so sorry. That sounded so callous. It's just...I mean...she can't wear it, you know?"

I did know, and I wasn't really sure what to do with it once I *did* finish, but that was a problem for another day. "One of her dying wishes," I said.

Tawny turned her pencil to the side, using the blunt side of the graphite to shade in the shape she'd drawn. "Wow, a dying wish. I've only ever seen those in the movies."

"Me, too," I said as I bent to pick up my totes and head to the art room.

She peered over the desk and through the plexiglass, suddenly jumping up. "Hey! Let me help you with those."

Before I could tell her I had it, she was by my side and

lightening my load by taking one of my bags. "Thanks, Tawny."

"Oh yeah, of course." We walked through the central meeting space. Art and ceramics from the various classes offered decorated the walls and shelves. Bliss had some talented folks.

"Maybe you can give it to her sister," Tawny said.

"What?"

"The dress you're painting. Maybe you can give it to Mary Lou."

"Or her daughter might like it. For a keepsake," I said, although Sue Ellen's death might be too fresh for Madison.

Tawny shook her head, her expression dismayed. "So sad."

It certainly was, and she didn't know the half of it.

Chapter Twelve

After Tawny left me in the classroom and returned to her station at the front desk, I watched the second hand of the analog clock on the wall as it made its circle with a grating *tick, tick, tick*. I hadn't noticed it before, but now, as I waited in the otherwise silent room, it was all I heard. The sound bored into my head like a woodpecker pecking against the siding of my farmhouse, but I couldn't pound the wall to make the pecking stop. I picked up a tube of acrylic paint, tossing it from one hand to the other. I raised my arm, seriously contemplating hurling the tube at the clock to make it stop, but Mary Lou shuffled in at that moment. She looked at my lifted arm and cocked a brow at me but didn't say anything. I dropped the tube with a thunk and jumped up. "I'm so glad you're here!"

"I have nowhere else to be," she said forlornly.

I knew from losing Meemaw how deep a feeling that was. The death of a loved one had a way of zapping all your energy and zest for life. Eventually, you got to the point where you decided to live again, but getting there could be an uphill climb. I resisted asking her how she was doing because it was obvious. She was miles worse than she'd been when I'd seen her last or how she'd sounded on the phone when I'd talked to her about Bennett Macaw. The pallor of her skin was pasty. Her hair hung limply, clinging to her head. Her shoulders slouched forward as if they carried the weight of the world.

I didn't want to, but I couldn't help thinking about the for sale sign in front of Four Peppers Ranch. It was definitely a motive, but could she really have orchestrated killing her sister over their family's property? I had no answer to that question.

I guided her to a table...not the one she had sat at before, which was adjacent to the one Sue Ellen had taken. I figured it would be better to change things up. She slumped down in the chair, dropping the bag she'd brought with her dress and paint supplies to the floor by her side. She looked up at me. "Any news?" she asked, just like Tawny had, only Mary Lou was asking in the context of potential murder, not the tragic early death of a woman due to heart failure.

"I'm afraid not," I said.

She scrunched her lips together like she had a mouthful of Sour Patch Gummies. After a weighty few seconds, she sighed. "Were you able to reach Bennett?"

"I'm meeting with him this afternoon. After our class is over." I went to my table and started unpacking my totes. Before long, the table was littered with tubes of paint, a stack of paper plates, paintbrushes, old cottage cheese and pint ice cream containers for water, and a roll of paper towels. I unfolded the dress I'd brought with me—Sue Ellen's dress— and laid it flat. Crystal and Yvette walked in. Just like Mary Lou, they were each more subdued than they'd been before Sue Ellen's death. "I had to drag myself here," Crystal said.

Yvette nodded her agreement. "I feel like an armadillo crossing the road but not giving a hoot whether it makes it or not."

I got it. Losing someone took a huge toll on the psyche under the best of circumstances. When that death was the result of murder? Well, that was a whole different ballgame. "Ladies," I said, "nothing's going to make the pain go away, but maybe we can get lost in painting, just for a little while."

Mary Lou squeezed her eyes shut and shook her head, making it clear she didn't believe it was possible to get lost in anything except her grief. Crystal crinkled her forehead but laid out the pale pink t-shirt she'd brought. Yvette pressed her lips together with such force that the olive skin around her mouth turned white, but like Crystal, she spread out her t-shirt on the table.

"Did you bring somethin', Mary Lou?" Crystal asked.

Mary Lou expelled a heavy breath but reached into her bag and withdrew a jean jacket. Rhinestones and embroidery already embellished the front. "Oh, a jacket! Just like Harlow's. Such a good idea. What're you gonna paint?" Crystal asked.

"Daisies," she said as she unfolded a sheet of paper. On it was a sketch of the mounded flower patch I'd seen the day before at Four Peppers Ranch. "Sue Ellen's favorites."

The ones she'd jokingly said to bury her under. I swallowed. At the time she'd said it, it had been in jest. Now, looking back, it felt foreboding. I pushed away the dark, lingering feeling of fingertips creeping up my spine and got us started, putting into practice the techniques we'd covered during the previous class. Over the next thirty minutes, the three women all slipped into their private thoughts as they painted the garments they'd brought. I circulated, helping them when they got stuck, giving advice on colors, and generally being a cheerleader. All I wanted to do was bolster them up and let them escape their pain for just a little while.

Tawny appeared in the doorway. "It's so slow in front. Mind if I take a look?" she asked.

"Sure," I said, beckoning her in.

She walked around, stopping at each table, taking the time

to really look at what each woman worked on. "They all look so great," she said. She stopped at my table. "You're not painting?"

I glanced at Sue Ellen's dress. "I was, but I think I'm going to work on it at home."

Tawny reached out and lightly touched the fabric with the pads of her fingers. "This is it, isn't it? Her dress? The one the deputy gave you?"

Crystal lifted her gaze from the shapes she was painting. "Whose dress?"

I started folding it up to put it back in the bag. "Sue Ellen's," I said. My fingers felt the bulk of the seam connecting the bodice to the skirt. It wasn't particularly well-made for actual couture. If Christian Dior could see it, he'd be turning in his grave. If Sue Ellen were alive, I'd take the whole thing apart and remake it for her. As it was, painting the flowers she'd drawn would have to be enough.

Mary Lou's head snapped up. "That's Sue's? How'd you get it?"

"Deputy McClaine brought it to me. It was in a bag at her house." I said.

She balked. "He should have given it to me!"

"It had a card with my name on it," I said, explaining.

As I held it up, Mary Lou jumped up, the chair legs scraping the floor from the force of the sudden movement. She started toward me, arms outstretched, and practically ripped the dress from my hands. She held it by the shoulder seams, staring at it. "It can't be..."

"What can't be?" I asked.

"This was Mother's," she said, her voice low and quiet.

"Betsy's?" Yvette asked.

Mary Lou's lips curved into a reminiscent smile. "She loved this dress. It's a Dior. I remember..."

Crystal circled around her table and came up next to Mary

Lou. She gently touched her shoulder. "What do you remember, honey?"

Mary Lou's hands fisted at the shoulder seams and she jerked her arms making the dress dance in the air. "This! I remember this!"

Crystal, Yvette, Tawny, and I all stared at Mary Lou, uncomprehending. She gaped at Crystal. "Don't you remember? She wore this to prom the year..." She paused. Closed her eyes and shook her head. "*That* year," she finished.

All the color drained from Crystal's face. Yvette dropped the paintbrushes she'd been holding and came to Mary Lou's other side. "She kept it? All these years?"

"Are you sure?" Crystal asked, peering to get a better look. "Are you sure it's the same dress?"

"It's definitely a Dior," I said, confirming what Mary Lou had said.

"Wait, what?" Tawny asked, looking completely bewildered.

Yvette turned to us, letting Crystal comfort Mary Lou. "Sue Ellen wore that dress to prom with her boyfriend. They broke up after that, and he left Bliss. She was so heartbroken."

"I can't believe she kept it," Mary Lou said again. Tears pooled in her eyes as she laid the dress over her arm and ran her fingertips over the flowers Sue Ellen had drawn onto the fabric and over the stems she'd started to paint.

"Daisies," she whispered, her fingertips brushing the petals of the drawn flowers.

I put my hand on Mary Lou's shoulder, wishing my charm could simply infuse her with strength. "She wanted you to finish painting it?" she asked me.

I nodded, then she nodded, pressing her lips together to hold back her emotions. She quickly folded the dress again and handed it back to me. She slipped out from under my touch and went back to her chair.

"How long will it take you to finish?" Crystal asked.

"A few days, I think. It's all sketched out. I started this morning. I'll work on it some more tonight. Or maybe this afternoon after my appointment with—" I broke off, kicking myself for nearly saying Bennett Macaw's name. Mary Lou knew, but the rest of them didn't need to know I was meeting with him. "After an...an appointment I have." And then, in my best teacher voice, I redirected them to their painting. Tawny scooted away and as unenthusiastic as the other three women were, they settled in and we continued with our class.

Chapter Thirteen

Like most things in Bliss, Texas Mineral Brokers was housed in an old building. It was situated two blocks off the square. Their sign was understated—just a metal plaque with the company's name in gold letters. Bennett Macaw's office was upstairs and had east-facing windows. Based on his early coffee fix, he struck me as the type who wanted morning sun. He ushered me in and I sat in one of the leather chairs facing his big mahogany desk.

He wasn't much for preamble and just launched right into the reason for our meeting—at least from his perspective. "I did a little research on your great-grandmother's house. 2112 Mockingbird Lane."

I sputtered, a tangle of knots low in my gut. I hadn't given him my address. "Wait, how did you know where I live?"

He must have sensed my confusion because he held up one hand, palm out as if to reassure me. "Don't worry, it's what I do, and the information is accessible to the public," he said with a laugh. "I looked up your name and found the property address. Once you have some basic information, it's easy to track down parcel numbers, look at ownership history, property taxes. Things like that. Looks like Loretta Mae Cassidy deeded the house to you—" He looked at his notes written on a pad of paper— "thirty-two years ago."

His explanation made sense and the knots in my stomach uncoiled. "That's right," I said. "When I was born."

He nodded with approval. "Seeing a property passed from generation to generation...well, it's nice. Meaningful."

It was. Maybe that's why Sue Ellen had never wanted to sell Four Peppers Ranch. Maybe she'd wanted to keep it in the family and pass it on to her children. I watched Bennett to see if I could detect anything beneath his words. Was he angry Mary Lou had listed the property for sale? Did he want it to go to his children? Of course, there was no way I could know without asking directly, which I couldn't do. I needed another way in.

Before I could think of one, he brought us back to my farmhouse. "The mineral rights for 2112 Mockingbird Lane transferred to you with the ownership of the house. As far as what they're worth, I can look into it for you."

I blinked. "What?"

He put his elbows on the desk and tented his hands, placing the tips of his fingers under his chin. "Unless the mineral rights are explicitly sold, and thereby excluded from a real estate contract, they transfer with the house. The mineral rights for 2112 Mockingbird Lane have never been sold, therefore the rights are yours. It's up to you if you want to sell them. You said you've been approached by a buyer. Who is it?"

I answered his question with one of my own, just out of curiosity. "How much are they worth?" I hadn't really cared about the mineral rights, but now I wondered what amount of money I was sitting on. More than that, I wondered what the mineral rights for Four Peppers Ranch might be worth.

And if Mary Lou planned to exclude those rights when she sold.

"That's a tough question," Bennett said. "Generally, until you sell, there's no way to know the exact value. But when we calculate them, we look at five things." He ticked them off on his fingers as he ran through them. "One, how many net mineral acres do you own? That's what payment is based on. The more net acres you own, the more you'll be paid. Two, what's the current royalty rate? Three, the price of oil and/or gas. Basically, you, the property owner, own the oil and gas below ground. As the price of oil and gas fluctuates, so, too, does the royalty rate. It's a little more stable as the rates for mineral rights are calculated based on a six-month average. Four, the royalty income you may be earning. The more you make if you are leasing those rights, the more a buyer will be willing to pay. And five, the potential income. There are different approaches to this. Some buyers don't put any value on future income. Others may be willing to pay millions. Either way, it's a crap shoot because no one actually knows what future earnings will look like."

"So the rights are just sitting there unless I'm leasing them?" I asked. This would apply to Four Peppers Ranch, too, assuming the rights hadn't been leased or sold and still belonged to the family.

"Exactly. If your mineral rights are not leased, they're what's called non-producing. You aren't earning any royalty income. If they *are* leased, you're earning off of that lease, and the potential sale price may be higher, depending on what you're earning. If your leased rights are producing, they're obviously worth more."

"When—or I guess *how*—do you know if you should sell or lease?" I asked.

He shrugged. "There's no one answer to that question, Ms. Cassidy. As I said, I can do some digging for you. See if any drilling is planned that will pull from your parcel. You don't own much land, though, so chances are you wouldn't earn much with a lease or sell for very much. On top of that, mineral buyers can be a shady bunch. It's an unfortunate truth. They take advantage of people's ignorance on a daily basis by severely undervaluing market value. If someone has approached you to sell, be wary of that offer. I'd bet my house that it's not a fair market value offer."

"It's a lot to think about," I said with complete sincerity, because it was, and I'd never even known it was a thing. Maybe in the periphery of my mind, but that was the extent of it.

"It is," Bennett said. He narrowed his eyes, peering at me. "Are you sure we haven't met?"

This was my opening. I gave a light laugh. "I don't know. I don't think so. Not unless you've needed a custom dress designed or signed up for a class at the Bliss Arts Center."

His placid expression turned into a frown. "The Arts Center?"

"Right. I'm teaching a fabric painting class there. That's what I was doing this morning."

"Sue Ellen was in that class," he said quietly.

"Sue Ellen Pepper-Mac—" I stopped and pressed my hand to my forehead as if I'd just had a realization. "Macaw. Oh my heavens, is…was Sue Ellen your…ex-wife?"

The force of his pressing his lips together drained the blood from the rim of his mouth and turned it white. "Yes. No. Well, we were separated, but not divorced. We were reconciling."

I sat up straighter, my spine crackling. "You were?" Mary Lou and Yvette had both said Sue Ellen and Bennett were divorced, not just separated. Long divorced, in fact. "For some reason, I thought Sue Ellen was divorced some time ago."

He closed his eyes for a beat. His nostrils flared as he drew in a steadying breath. It looked as if talking about Sue Ellen wasn't easy for him. Either he was an exceptional, award-winning actor, or he was really distraught. I'd learned many things from Meemaw over the years, but one thing always stuck out. Never miss an occasion to close your mouth and open your ears. I'd found that to be particularly true when it came to digging into the whys and hows of a murder. People filled the silent space you left, so I had learned to leave plenty of it. Now I let Bennett Macaw talk."We could never bring ourselves to sign the papers," he said. "People assumed and we just never corrected them. It's nobody's business, right? We tried living apart, but...in the end, we decided we didn't like it. We didn't want to drag the kids through our ups and downs, though. Not until we were sure. The separation's been hard on them. And now this. Sue Ellen's death..."

He turned around in his chair to gather his emotions.

I thought back to when I'd glimpsed Bennett in the hospital, and even this morning at Villa Farina. His eyes were bloodshot and his face was drawn like he was grieving. I also thought about seeing him at Four Peppers Ranch. He'd been dealing with some conflict. He'd said that something was impossible. If only I could come straight out and ask him.

"I'm so sorry for your loss," I said, and I meant it, but I also had a new theory about Sue Ellen's death. If they had still been married, and he was the beneficiary and inherited her part of Four Peppers Ranch, then that was a pretty good reason to kill. And if there were millions of dollars of mineral rights involved in the ownership of the acreage? Well, that drove the motive home. I needed to get out of here, get home, and do some sewing so that I could think. It was going to be a late night.

Chapter Fourteen

The porch at 2112 Mockingbird Lane held two rocking chairs painted white. As I walked through the arbor that marked the entrance to my yard and up the flagstone path, I saw that one of the rockers moved back and forth in a steady rhythm. The other sat still as a statue. As I climbed the steps to the porch, I directed my gaze to the chair in motion and said, "Hey, Meemaw." I knew from experience that if I sat in the chair Meemaw currently inhabited, I would be enveloped in a cocoon of warmth that felt like being wrapped up in a heated blanket. Given that it was a toasty eight-seven degrees out, with humidity at about ninety percent, I opted to sit in the chair that wasn't currently occupied by a ghost.

I glanced at the air space Meemaw occupied and saw a shimmering shape beginning to take form. As I watched, the air rippled and flickered, becoming a little clearer for a moment before fading back to nothing. We were working on it, but at this point, Meemaw still couldn't communicate with me by talking. She managed to find other ways, whether through clanging pipes, the torn pages of my fashion magazines, or writing on a steamed-up mirror. She was inventive, but so far, no dice. Not yet, anyway. I knew we'd have a breakthrough, though...one of these days.

Communication notwithstanding, her presence was mostly enough for me. Knowing she was still with me on this side of the veil filled me with comfort I hadn't known I needed. Mama was my rock—no doubt about that—but she was in her honeymoon phase with Hoss. She and Nana still came around just as much as they ever did, but the sheriff was in tow more often than he used to be, which changed the dynamic of the Cassidy women's gatherings. I liked it when Meemaw, Nana, Mama, and I were all together. Four generations of Cassidy women under one roof. When Gracie was there, it was a bonus.

I didn't want Meemaw to ever go away, and one of my goals was to help her figure out how to take a more corporeal form so that maybe she could stay forever. So far, we hadn't succeeded at that. The clearest look I'd gotten of her was a faint glimpse of her plaid shirt with snap buttons and jeans. It was the same type of clothing Nana lived in. That apple hadn't fallen far from the tree.

As long as the chair rocked, I knew Meemaw was still next to me. "What are you doing out here?" I asked her.

Her response was to make the screen door bang as if a gust of wind had caught it. I still hadn't figured out how she managed to be in two ghostly places at once. Here she was, the chair still rocking, but also throwing her spectral weight around five feet away. "Ah, change of scenery—" I started, but the screen door creaked open again and crashed closed with an echoing thwack. I jumped, suddenly on alert. "What is it, Meemaw?"

Again and again and again the screen door slammed. Something was wrong inside the house, I realized. I leaped up and two seconds later I grabbed the screen door, threw open the main door, and raced into Buttons & Bows.

And I stopped dead in my tracks because things were not as they should be. The magazine rack lay on the ground, every fashion magazine and my lookbooks scattered across the floor. The ready-to-wear rack was pulled out from the wall. Pieces from the collection hung haphazardly from their hangers. The velvet settee had been pushed against the coffee table. Even the doors of the antique armoire that Will had helped move down from the attic had been ripped open, the stacks and stacks of fabric strewn about.

I slowly turned and walked from the showroom portion of the house, aka the living room, to my atelier, aka the dining room. I held my breath, afraid of what I might find. Meemaw's old Singer sewing machine was in there, along with my PFAFF and Baby Lock serger, and three dress forms with garments in varying states of completion. More than that, though, there were jars and jars and jars of buttons and other sewing detritus on shelves.

All I could do was stare. Only a few of the jars had been knocked over. One had broken. Buttons and snaps and pieces of thick glass spilled across the floor. I breathed a sigh of relief. It could have been so much worse. I scanned the rest of the room, the anxiety that had pooled in my chest releasing. The sewing machines were fine, all upright and undisturbed. But then my breath hitched. One of the dress forms was naked. The dress from that had held Sue Ellen's partially painted vintage dress, which I'd hung there before my meeting with Bennett Macaw.

I laced my fingers together and pressed them to the top of my head. "*Ohmygod, ohmygod, ohmygod.*" I sounded just like Mary Lou had in the parking lot of the Arts Center after Sue Ellen had collapsed. I had to finish painting that dress. I *had* to! It was a dying woman's last wish. I took a breath then bellowed, "Meemaw!"

A gust of warm air shot through me and I screeched,

stumbling. I caught myself and straightened. Passing through my body like that was one of her new parlor tricks and I hated it. It felt as if all the cells of my physical self were momentarily disrupted—scattered out of place like all the buttons and glass on the floor. It took a few uncomfortable seconds and a few deep breaths to reorient myself. "Loretta Mae Cassidy," I scolded, using her full name.

The pipes in the walls creaked in a rhythmic pattern that sounded like laughter.

"What happened?" I asked, stifling my agitation with her tricks. "Where's Sue Ellen's dress?"

The air in the house whipped into a gentle cyclone, not powerful enough to do any more damage to the current state of things but strong and isolated enough to force me into motion. My feet almost lifted fully from the ground, as if I were walking on a stream of air. The invisible energy Meemaw generated propelled me up the stairs, into my bedroom, and then through the door which led to the attic. The air in the room was still and heavy with concentrated heat. I blinked away my momentary disorientation and gasped when I saw why Meemaw had brought me up here. There, on a dress form I had yet to bring downstairs, was the vintage Dior, safe and sound.

Chapter Fifteen

Mama and Nana stood side by side in the kitchen, looking past the threshold to the atelier in all its disarray. "You need to call Hoss," Mama said. She tapped her booted foot. Come hell or high water, Mama always wore cowboy boots. She'd even gotten herself a special pair of white boots, which she'd blinged up with rhinestones, for her wedding. She saved those for special occasions and date nights with her new hubby.

Nana was the complete opposite. The moment she entered my house—almost always through the Dutch door in the kitchen—she kicked off her Crocs and padded around in her pristine white socks. She was a goat-whisperer, but I wondered if she had a secondary charm and if that charm was the ability to keep her socks looking brand new no matter what puddle of mud or cloud of dirt she may have stepped in along the way. If Nana actually did have a secondary charm, it wasn't so far-fetched to think that I did, too. But I didn't want to think about that right now. "I am not calling Hoss, because he might be inclined to send Gavin instead."

Mama gave me the full force of her frown. "And?"

"He may be your stepson now," I said, "but he's not my friend."

"Maybe not, but he is your stepbrother...*and* he's the deputy sheriff, so you're gonna need to figure out how to work with him. Especially since you keep gettin' yourself involved in death and murder."

I grumbled under my breath. She was right on both counts.

"So someone was looking for Sue Ellen's dress?" Nana asked.

"I don't know. It's not like Meemaw can answer that question," I said, but it seemed probable. Why else would someone have broken in here, number one, and number two, why would Meemaw have hidden the dress from the intruder?

I went upstairs to retrieve Sue Ellen's dress from the attic. When I was halfway back down the stairs, I could see that my entire house was in mayhem. Again. Meemaw was working her magic. In the atelier, all the buttons and bits of trims that had been all over the floor spun around like a tornado, and then, as if she flicked her invisible wrist, everything suddenly flew back into its place. In the front room, the magazines and hangers and the pieces of clothing that had been strewn across the floor were in motion, circling and circling and circling. Just like in my sewing room, in a split second, everything shot like bullets to the places they belonged.

I heard a loud, sharp gasp from the front door and my heart flipped in my chest. Someone had come into Buttons & Bows in the midst of Meemaw's magic. Good lord, I hoped it wasn't Gavin. I hurried down the remaining steps and turned, stopping short when I saw Madelyn. She cupped one hand over her forehead, her mouth curved into a toothy smile. "That. Was. Brilliant," she said. Even though she's said only three little words, her English accent was distinct.

Relief instantly flooded me. "Oh, thank God it's you!" I

tossed Sue Ellen's dress over my shoulder and doubled over, bracing my hands on my knees so my heartbeat could simmer down. I didn't know if Meemaw didn't understand that she needed to keep her presence on the down low, or if she just didn't care. My guess was probably the latter. She had been a rule-breaker her entire life. Just because she now lived in the spirit world didn't mean that trait had gone away. I'd have to have a chat with her later. If it had been Gavin walking in—or some other unsuspecting customer—instead of Madelyn, I'd be doing ten-gallon hat-sized damage control.

"You okay, love?" she asked, coming to me and placing her hand on my back.

I stood and waved my hand around. "Yeah, yeah. You gave me a fright, is all. I mean Meemaw, and—" I waved my arm around haphazardly— "all this..."

She put her palm to her chest, still beaming. "Bill's going to be so jealous when I tell him what I witnessed. Oh my goodness. I just...I came at the perfect moment."

I skirted around her and closed the front door, then slid the dress from my shoulder. For the second time, I felt something hard just above the seam between the bodice and the skirt. Every single part of a Dior should have been perfect. That's part of what couture was about, after all. The silhouettes were clean and distinct and beautiful. There was no room for an error in workmanship like this.

I gripped the hard knot as Madelyn and I headed back into the atelier. My fingers danced across the layers of fabric creating the seam. In the atelier, Madelyn peppered Mama and Nana with questions about Meemaw's magic, but I sat down at Meemaw's old Singer and turned the dress inside out. I examined it. Starting at the center, I tapped the pads of my fingers against the layers of the seam until I made my way all the way around, but it was only that one spot that was bulky. That's when I saw it. A one and half-inch section where the original stitching had been ripped out and inexpert slip-stitching had closed it up again. I found a gap between the stitches and poked one finger into the space. One of the long slip-stitches broke and suddenly the entire section that had been re-sewn came apart. And inside the space between the fabric and the facing of the bodice, I found something. I must have made some sort of sound because Mama, Nana, and Madelyn had stopped their conversation and now watched me. I dug my fingers into the opening and a second later, pulled out a gold ring tied to a narrow strip of white grosgrain ribbon.

We all stared at it, and I imagined we all had the same questions racing through our minds. Why had this piece of jewelry been hidden in the bodice of Sue Ellen's old prom dress? But in an instant, I knew the answer. It had to be the promise ring Christopher had given to Sue Ellen before they'd broken up.

I hung the dress back on the dress form, studying it. Looking at the ring, then back to the dress. "What is it, darlin'?" Mama asked, sidling up to me.

It was too many things. Was it the dress someone wanted when they'd broken into my shop, or did someone know about what had been hidden inside? My suspicion instantly flew to Mary Lou. She'd recognized the Dior. Her shock that Sue Ellen had kept it was real. Had she known about the ring? But it was just a gold promise ring. It was sentimental to Sue Ellen, but it didn't look particularly valuable.

"I'm trying to figure out why Sue Ellen wanted me to have this dress. Did she want me to find the ring?"

"You'd have to figure out why that ring was there in the first place to answer that, I imagine," Mama said.

Right. I kept talking, processing aloud. "She left the hospital after she'd had a heart attack, went home, and put this dress in a bag with my name on it. But why?"

"That *is* curious," Madelyn said. "So curious."

"Curiouser still," Nana said, "because it seems that someone interrupted her and killed her."

But was that how it played out? "Maybe *she* interrupted someone who was already there," I said. "And if she had, did she manage to put this dress in the bag with my name before confronting whoever it was?"

"Why would she do that, darlin'?" Mama asked.

That was the question I'd been mulling over since Gavin had brought me the dress. I'd only been able to land on one reason. I spoke slowly, wondering if it would sound crazy spoken aloud. "What if she was trying to tell me something?"

Madelyn gasped. Nodded enthusiastically. "Like who killed her, you mean?!"

"It's possible. That doesn't answer the question of why she left the hospital—"

Mama spiraled her hand in the air, cutting me off. "Let's not think about that right now. She did. She left. Who knows why, but she did."

"Right," Madelyn said. "Maybe if we figure out what she was trying to tell you with the dress—or the ring, the rest will fall into place."

We moved through the French doors into the kitchen. Madelyn and I sat at the table while Mama and Nana took out glasses from the cupboard and filled them with ice and water. They each carried two, Mama handing her second glass to me and Nana handing hers to Madelyn. The cupboard, which Mama had shut, suddenly creaked open and the glasses on the shelf rattled. "Aw, Meemaw, I wish you could have yourself a glass of water with us," I said.

Madelyn blinked, then blinked again. She rotated her head, scanning the airspace of the kitchen as if she were hoping to catch a glimpse of Meemaw's spectral self. "Oh my, I wish you could, too," she said, gaze directed to the cabinet Loretta Mae had been rattling around in a few seconds before.

As if in response, the potted golden Pothos sitting in the center of the table jerked. It was as if an invisible rope was tied to it and someone started pulling it from one side of the table to the other. Madelyn caught the movement from the corner of her eye. She turned her head slowly, staring, her mouth in a surprised O shape. Without moving any other part of her body, she calmly placed her hands, palms down, on the table, then she cupped them, lightly touching the table with her fingertips as if they were resting on a Ouija Board. "Loretta Mae Cassidy, is that you?" she asked, her voice low and monotone as if she was afraid any emotion would scare my great-grandmother away.

The plant jerked, this time in Madelyn's direction. Her fingers flinched. She kept her face calm but a rosy glow shone from under her warm umber skin. The dusting of freckles across her nose seemed to darken. A second later, the curtains under the sink danced, then a stream of water flowed from the sink's faucet. Madelyn whipped her head around so fast I was afraid she might get whiplash. Her voice dropped to an amazed whisper. "She's speedy."

That she was. She could be flying through the pipes, making them clank, one second, then wreaking havoc in the attic the next. The spirit world, at least as far as the Cassidy women were concerned, did not have discernible rules. We sat in silence for a solid minute...maybe two...but there was no more sign of Meemaw. Madelyn heaved a sigh. "She's gone, isn't she?"

"Only for now," I said because if there was one thing I could count on, it was that Loretta Mae Cassidy would be back.

She'd be back. That phrase echoed in my mind. Mary Lou had uttered it when she'd been here. What had we been talking about? I racked my brain, and then it hit me. She'd been talking about the threatening letters Sue Ellen had gotten and the one she'd seen. "I'll be back soon," I muttered. Was whoever sent those letters after the dress or the ring?

I returned to the question of why Sue Ellen had left the hospital that night. What if whoever it was *had* come back...in person this time. Could it have been a setup? Someone may have told her to go home...threatened her—maybe even to give them the dress—or something bad would happen. To who? Her? Her children? Her sister? The more I thought about it, the more it made sense. But then again, I reasoned, she'd been carefully watched by the hospital staff. Only her family...and I...had been allowed in to see her. And if the dress was there in the bag all along, whoever killed her would have found it, right?

The entire day replayed like scenes from a movie in my head. I'd been talking with Tawny. Driving away from the Arts Center. A scream. I'd hightailed it over to where Mary Lou, Crystal, Yvette, and Sue Ellen were. Sue Ellen lay on the ground clutching her heart.

My mind stuttered. Oh! "She had something in her hand," I said.

Mama, Nana, and Madelyn swiveled their heads to look at me. "Sue Ellen," I clarified. "When she left our fabric painting class that day, she had all her stuff in a bag, except a sheet of paper. She was holding it when she walked out."

Madelyn blinked and leaned forward. "You think it might have been one of the threatening letters?"

"Maybe," I said, letting my thoughts solidify. If it was and if it had threatened someone she loved, or told her to do something at home, that could have been reason enough to leave the hospital.

Another question surfaced: What had happened to that sheet of paper?

Chapter Sixteen

"If she had it when she collapsed, but not when she got to the hospital, then what happened to it?" I asked aloud, then continued my musings. "Mary Lou, Crystal, and Yvette were the only ones with her."

I thought about the break-in again, too. The same three women knew that I had Sue Ellen's dress. They'd all been there when Sue Ellen had collapsed. Any one of them could have taken the paper Sue Ellen had been clutching in her hand.

"If it *was* one of the letters, why would they do that and not say anything?"

That was a good question.

A sudden tapping on the kitchen window drew me out of my thoughts. Thelma Louise stood on the other side of the glass, her big eyes looking at me like she was staring me down. "What'd'ya want?" I asked, looking the goat straight in the eyes.

As she gave a slow blink, Nana jumped up and shooed the goat away.

I'd met Thelma Louise's gaze head-on. *Head-on.* That's

what I needed to do now. I needed to call one of the women to get the answer from the goat's mouth, so to speak. I wasn't sure if I could trust Mary Lou anymore. She'd put the family ranch up for sale the second Sue Ellen was gone. She, of anyone, had a connection to the dress. It had belonged to her mother and Sue Ellen had kept it from her.

I hadn't formed much of a relationship with Crystal, so I turned to Yvette. We'd spent time together in Buttercup and at Four Peppers Ranch. Of the three of them, she was the one I felt comfortable asking. I pulled up her contact information in my phone and dialed. She answered on the third ring with a surprised, "Hello? Harlow?"

"Hey, Yvette," I said. I dispensed with the Southern hospitality Mama expected of me then cut to the chase. "Do you remember if Sue Ellen had a letter or a sheet of paper with her when...when she had the heart attack in the parking lot?"

"Paper?" she repeated.

"Yeah. I seem to remember that she took it out of her tote bag when she was leaving class. I have a distinct memory of it being in one of her hands when I ran up. In the confusion of the paramedics arriving and taking her, I completely forgot about it."

Yvette was quiet for a solid ten seconds. I heard the faint drumming of her fingertips on a hard surface. "Now that you mention it, I kind of do remember that," she said slowly. "What happened to it?" she mused.

"I've been trying to remember if someone took it. One of the paramedics?"

"If they did, it would be with her stuff, right?"

Right. "Where *is* her stuff?" I asked.

"I don't kn—" She broke off and paused, then blurted, "Oh, Wait! I think...Mary Lou went in the ambulance, right? So...I think Crystal took the bag...yes! That's right. I remember. Some of the stuff fell out when Sue Ellen collapsed. When the paramedics were getting her into the ambulance, I think Crystal picked it up and put it all back in the bag. Yes. I'm sure of it."

"Do you think she gave it to Mary Lou?"

"Hang on," Yvette said. "Lemme text her."

I waited, clutching the phone between my ear and shoulder, tapping my fingers on the table. She came back on the line thirty seconds later. "She said it's still in her car."

A bolt of energy shot through me. If Sue Ellen dropped the crumpled paper, Crystal may have grabbed it with the rest of the things that had spilled from Sue Ellen's bag. "Yvette, can you ask her if I can come get it?"

"Hang on," she said. I waited while she sent another text. After another long thirty seconds, she came back. "She said she can meet you at the Arts Center in thirty minutes."

My heart nearly pounded out of my chest. This could be the answer to why Sue Ellen left the hospital and headed straight into her murderer's web.

I hid the ring in one of the Mason jars of buttons. For decades, a jar just like that had hidden the ring Butch Cassidy had given to Texana, and which now sat on my ring finger. It felt as good a place to hide the promise ring as any. If it...or the dress...had been the object of the burglary, well, whoever had broken in knew it wasn't here. Plus Meemaw *was* here and she had skills. If a second attempt was made, she'd be able to thwart it once again.

Thirty minutes crept by. Mama and Nana left, but Madelyn stayed. I knew she hoped she'd catch another glimpse of Meemaw. I left her in the gathering room and I went back to my atelier. I perched on a stool in front of Sue Ellen's dress and talked to myself under my breath, wishing *her* ghost would appear by Meemaw's side. It didn't work like that though. Instead of getting answers that way, I stared at the Dior. Blades of grass sprouted from the hemline. From there, bursts of daisies danced on the skirt. It was a lovely design, inspired by her love of gardening and the flower garden at Four Peppers Ranch. What was it about daisies that had enamored Sue Ellen so?

"Let's go."

Madelyn's voice snapped me from my thoughts. I clapped my hands. It was time. "Right!"

Ten minutes later, and five minutes early, we were at the lobby of the Arts Center chatting with Tawny, waiting for Crystal. She plowed through the door, a large tote in hand, which I recognized as Sue Ellen's. "Sorry I'm late!"

I glanced at the clock. "You're not," I said. It took every ounce of strength not to charge her like a bull at a rodeo and snatch that red bag from her hands. Finally, she held it out to me. "With everything happening, I forgot I had this. You'll take it to Mary Lou?"

"Sure will," I said. I caught Madelyn's gaze and nodded toward the door. We could look through the bag once we were back in Buttercup.

"Leaving already?" Tawny asked.

"Things to do," I said.

"I get it." She cleared her throat. "I was just, um, thinking. I thought we could do something special in honor of Sue Ellen at your last class."

Crystal's eyes brightened. "Oh! *She* would have loved that. It can be our own special memorial," Crystal said. "Maybe we can wear our t-shirts."

"What a lovely idea," Madelyn said, nodding her approval.

Tawny smiled, looking pleased.

"I guess I better go home and finish painting," Crystal said.

As Tawny reached her hand through the little opening at the base of the plexiglass, I caught a glimpse of her wall of photos and the memorial frame for the man she'd lost. She understood grief and now she was helping others process it. Maybe I could create a similar keepsake about Sue Ellen and give it to her children. I took her hand and squeezed, smiling at her. "It's a lovely idea, Tawny, thank you."

She waved as we left. I thought Crystal would head out, but she moved to the center between me and Madelyn. I slowed and caught Madelyn's eyes again. She winked and scooted between me and Crystal. "Thanks again for meeting us, love," she said, and she guided Crystal away.

Crystal got the message. "Home to paint!" she said, and she waved as she headed to her car.

In the cab of the truck, I dug into Sue Ellen's bag. I pulled out small containers of fabric paint—green, brown, white, and yellow. All the colors needed for Sue Ellen's field of flowers on the Dior. In class, she'd been painting a t-shirt—her practice piece. I took it from the bag and shook it open.

"She really loved daisies, didn't she?" Madelyn said.

"She really did," I said. She really, *really* did. Without warning, a thread of memory tried to surface in the corner of my mind. I tried to grab ahold of it, but it hung just out of reach so I let it go.

The piece of paper I'd been searching for was at the bottom of the bag, crushed even more from the weight of a rectangular plastic storage box holding Sue Ellen's paint brushes and tubes of acrylic paint. My heart skittered with anticipation. Madelyn sucked in a breath and I held mine as I carefully took the paper by the edges. I placed it on the flat surface of the storage box and plucked a tissue from the box I kept in the cab, using it to flatten out the crumpled page. Just like Mary Lou had described the letter she'd seen, this one was written like a dramatic ransom note with cutouts of letters and words. I read it aloud.

> Time is up.
> Your house. 12 midnight.
> Or I will tell the world what you've kept buried all these years.

Madelyn and I gasped at the same time. This paper held the clue as to why Sue Ellen left the hospital. I snapped my hands away. I'd been careful, but I didn't want to risk contaminating the page with even a smidgeon of my fingerprints. This was so much worse than I ever could have imagined. "We have to call Gavin," I said, already scrolling through my phone's contact list to find his number.

I told him what we'd found. He gave an exasperated sigh but somehow held in the frustration I knew he had about the fact that I—rather than him—had found a significant clue. "I'll be there in ten minutes," he said. "Sit tight."

My heart thundered in my chest. "No problem," I told him. I hardly wanted to move for fear of having my own heart attack.

That fear brought up an image of Sue Ellen on the ground in this very parking lot, but then something else came to me. That hadn't been her first episode. Just after we'd moved classrooms, she'd gone pale and put her palm to her chest like she was having pains. It had happened so spontaneously. Or had it? Had there been a trigger?

I racked my brain, trying to remember, letting the scene play out in my mind. I'd been unpacking my supplies. The four women—Crystal, Yvette, Mary Lou, and Sue Ellen—had been chattering and setting up their own workstations. Where did the threatening letters come from? Had another one arrived that day? Had Sue Ellen pulled it out of her bag? Had *that* triggered the cardiac incident?

I came back to the movie playing in my head, but I just

couldn't remember if Sue Ellen had anything other than her paints and a t-shirt. Tawny had helped me with my things. She'd walked around, talking with the women before going back to the front desk. Then Sue Ellen pressed her hand to at her heart.

I stopped. Wait. Was that the order of things?

The scene moved backward as if I'd hit rewind. The women had been talking. Laughing. Setting up. Tawny had walked around. She's stopped to talk to Sue Ellen. *That's* when Sue Ellen went pale. *While* she was talking to Tawny, not after.

What had they talked about? Had Tawny wanted to call the paramedics? Oh God, could her heart attack have been prevented if we'd called 911? But no. Tawny had suggested it but Sue Ellen had refused. It wouldn't have saved her life in the end given that she died at her home, but I couldn't help but wonder if Sue Ellen knew about her heart condition. If she knew, why didn't she have nitroglycerine pills? Why wouldn't she want us to get her help?

I wanted to know what Sue Ellen and Tawny had talked about just before Sue Ellen clutched her heart. I jumped out of the truck and started to run back to the Arts Center.

"Harlow? Wait!" Madelyn said, hurling herself out of the truck after me.

"Stay with the letter!" I hollered over my shoulder. A few seconds later, I flew inside. Tawny yelped with surprise and jumped up. She stared at me. "What's wrong? Is someone hurt?"

I patted the air. "No, no, no." I paused to catch my breath. "I have...a question. That... first day of class, you helped me move classrooms." I gulped in some air. "Do you remember?"

She nodded, her spiky hair bouncing, the crow's feet around her eyes creating deep crevices. "Yeah, of course."

"Do you remember when you were talking to everyone,

looking at what they were going to paint? And Sue Ellen...it looked like...like she was having chest pains. Like something was wrong with her then. Did you notice that?"

The rosiness left Tawny's cheeks and the lines around her eyes carved in even deeper as she squinted, remembering. "God, yeah. She scared me to death. I asked her if I should call 911. I thought she was going to keel over—" She stopped. Gasped. "On my God, I didn't mean that."

I waved away her apology. "Did you notice anything?"

She looked at me puzzled. "What do you mean?"

"It was just so sudden. Did she...was she reading a letter or anything? Did someone say something? I'm just wondering what triggered it."

Tawny just shrugged helplessly. "Not that I remember," she said. "Maybe her heart was acting up already?"

"Yeah," I said with a sigh. "That's probably it."

"People ignore the signs," Tawny said. "It happens all the time, right?"

"I guess," I said. I felt defeated, as if I'd been one step away from discovering something vital, only to be yanked back. Deep down I thought there had to be more to it. *Something* triggered Sue Ellen's heart failure, but it was something I just wasn't seeing.

Chapter Seventeen

Gavin repeated the lines of the letter three times before looking at me and Madelyn. "Small towns and their secrets," he said with a shake of his head.

"Yeah," I said slowly. Sue Ellen had been obsessed with gardening, specifically with her daisies. She'd drawn daisies on the Dior dress she'd left me to finish, but why? She was dead. She'd asked to see me and told me she wanted to talk more once she was out of the hospital. She told me at the first fabric painting class that she had wanted to meet me, not because of my fashion design business but because I'd had a hand in solving some murders.

The ring. I kept coming back to the ring. And to those dratted daisies.

I circled back to the partial note and the dress she'd left for me.

Harlow, it needs to come out. Ch—

All along I'd been thinking she was referring to the chalk on the dress. That she wanted me to get it out of the fabric.

But what if that's *not* what it was about? What if it was about the ring? The ring needed to come out of its hiding place.

But why? And what was I supposed to do with it? I looked at the letter Gavin still held in his gloved hands.

> Time is up.
> Your house. 12 midnight.
> Or I will tell the world what you've kept buried all these years.

I ran through my theories. The first was that Mary Lou wanted the mineral rights to the land, but while that might be true, was that a motive to kill her sister? Their difference in opinion on selling their family ranch certainly was. They'd had a little squabble about it at our first fabric painting class. They'd talked about Sue Ellen's love of daisies, something I'd seen a lot of evidence of. Crystal had said something about the daisies at the ranch and Sue Ellen had said...what had she said? That nothing else would ever go there. That's why she wouldn't ever sell.

That had led to the bickering with Mary Lou, and with Sue Ellen saying she didn't want anyone tearing up the yard. Digging up what they'd planted there.

It has to come out. That's what Sue Ellen has written to me in her last moments. Not the chalk. Not even the ring.

I gasped. *A secret.*

What did the *Ch*— refer to? Again, not chalk. Another strand of a memory tickled my brain. Something Yvette had said. I walked away from Gavin and Madelyn, called up her number, and dialed. Once again, Mama's pleasantries went out the window and I just blurted out my question. "When we were at Four Peppers Ranch, you said Sue Ellen had a boyfriend before Bennett. I can't remember his name."

"Christopher," she said.

My stomach plummeted. Christopher. *Ch—* "Where is he now?"

"After they broke up, he left Bliss. I don't know what happened to him. I know the McVies thought he ran away at first, but I remember there was some...concern."

"What do you mean?"

"Like maybe he'd gotten in a car accident, or something. I mean, he never came back home."

A secret. The idea raced through my mind. What if Sue Ellen had a secret she didn't want to keep anymore? I turned and scanned the parking lot. My gaze settled on the Arts Center. *What if...*

As I made my way back to Gavin and Madelyn, my mind felt like Buttons & Bows looked when Meemaw had spun everything into a tornado before snapping her invisible fingers and making everything zip into its rightful place. "Oh my God," I whispered.

"What?" Madelyn asked.

I hung up on Yvette and called up the search engine on my phone and clumsily typed in the two names crowding my thoughts along with *Bliss, Texas.*

The entries popped up. I quickly scanned the first one and my blood ran cold. Right there, in black and white on the digital screen of my phone, my question was answered.

I looked at Gavin and Madelyn. My hand clamped around my stepbrother's arm and my head pounded. It seemed too outlandish. But it also made a weird kind of sense. Sue Ellen cared for those flowers. She wouldn't let anything happen to that flower bed. Yvette had said that after the breakup with Christopher, she'd become obsessed with the daisies. I told Gavin and Madelyn about Sue Ellen's boyfriend and how he'd vanished. "What if he didn't just disappear? What if he... *died*?"

"By died, you mean...killed?" Gavin clarified, his tone skeptical.

"Stranger things happen all the time." Madelyn nodded thoughtfully. "She was ready for the secret to come out."

I looked at the letter again:

Time is up.

Your house. 12 midnight.

Or I will tell the world what you've kept buried all these years.

"What you've kept buried all these years," I read. "Not figuratively. *Literally*. Under the daisies."

We fell silent. Movement in the parking lot caught my attention. The class that had been in session was over and the people filed out of the Arts Center, snippets of their conversations reaching us. Tawny was the last to leave. She punched a code into the keypad then walked next door and into the pizza place.

"I know what happened. I think I know who killed Sue Ellen."

Gavin stared at me, flabbergasted. "What?"

I held up one finger and grabbed my phone from the front seat of Buttercup. A second later, the phone rang and another second later, Bennett Macaw answered.

I put the phone on speaker. "Bennett, I'm going to ask you something. Don't ask me any questions right now. Just answer. I'll explain later."

He scoffed. "I don't think so—" he started, but Gavin grabbed my wrist and pulled it close to his face. "This is Deputy Gavin McClaine. Answer her damned question."

Bennett was a lawyer and wasn't easily intimidated—not even by the deputy sheriff. "What the hell's going on?" he demanded.

"That's a question," Gavin snapped. He looked at me. "What d'ya wanna know?"

I couldn't believe it was possible, but it was the only thing that made sense. "I was at Four Peppers Farm with Yvette the other day when you were—"

"What the—"

"Mr. Macaw!" Gavin snapped.

"You were there," I continued. "We saw your truck. We heard you on the phone." I recalled his side of the conversation. *"It's impossible. She would have told me,"* then, *"You are so off base."* He had to have been talking about the secret Sue Ellen had been keeping. Discounting it. But I thought I knew who'd been on the other end of the phone. And who'd sent the letters to Sue Ellen with the words and letters cut from magazines and newspapers. I knew because of a memorial photograph and a ring and a mound of daisies and those letters. And *Ch*—. "Who were you talking to?"

"Some crazy woman," he snapped.

"The name, Macaw," Gavin snapped right back, but I didn't need him to tell me who he'd been talking to. "It was Tawny McVie," I said.

Gavin and Madelyn stared at me and over the airwaves, Bennett Macaw blanched. "How did you know—"

"She thinks her brother's body is buried out there at the ranch," I whispered, my voice hoarse from the realization. I whipped my head around to look at the pizza place Tawny had sauntered into a few minutes ago. Even from where we stood, I could see her shape through the window staring at us. Gavin didn't need any more explanation. As much as I knew it grated on him, he also knew I was right. He might not have stitched the pattern pieces together, but he could be the one to take down a killer. He launched himself into a sprint like a runner coming off the blocks at a hundred-yard sprint.

At the same moment, Tawny flew through the door of the

pizza place and took off across the parking lot. I didn't bother to join the chase because she was no match for Gavin. He cut right, intercepting her before she was even halfway to her car. She tried to change directions but he juked, tricking her. Her feet twisted under her and she went down like a bullfighter who'd lost in the rodeo arena. Her angry screech echoed through the parking lot.

We watched the scene play out like it was a movie with a completely satisfying ending. Gavin hauled Tawny up and cuffed her, then read her Miranda rights as he dragged her toward us. "It's not my fault!" she screeched. "Sue Ellen...she told me what happened to Chris and then she...she just collapsed. It was like the secret was keeping her alive!"

"What happened?" Gavin said. "What happened with your brother?"

Tawny's chin quivered right alongside her voice. "He was bucked from a horse and he...he..."

"He died," I said.

She let out a sob. "She said he broke his neck. And then her daddy, that bastard, he shot the horse and he...he...buried my brother out there on the ranch."

I balked. "But it was an accident! Why did he do that? Why hide it?"

"So Christopher's family wouldn't sue him," she spat. "So *we* wouldn't take his ranch."

Oh my God. "And Sue Ellen knew," I said, sadness welling inside me. She'd had to live with that secret all these years. She'd kept the vintage Dior dress she'd worn to prom. She'd hidden the promise ring Christopher had given her. She'd told me in the note that the secret had to come out.

I thought again about the first heart incident in the Arts Center classroom. "She read your name tag, didn't she? She saw your last name, and then she saw the memorial photo of your brother." I thought about the threatening letters. The reference to revealing what Sue Ellen had kept buried all these years. "Did you know what had happened to him? To Christopher?" I asked Tawny.

"I guessed," she said with a sob. "He wouldn't have just disappeared, and he loved her. He wanted to marry her, so the story that they broke up never made sense. But I was just a teenager. No one listened to me."

"Did the authorities look into his disappearance?" Madelyn asked.

Tawny scoffed. "For about two seconds. They thought he skipped town because of Sue Ellen."

Gavin shook his head. Inside, I knew he was thanking God that his daddy, Hoss, hadn't been part of the sheriff's department back then. That he wasn't part of a botched investigation into a missing young man.

He put his hand on her head and started to guide her into the back seat of his patrol cruiser but I stopped him. "Why'd you break into my house?"

She angled her head to look at me, her expression completely defeated. "When I saw the dress and Mary Lou said Sue Ellen had worn it to prom, I don't know, something just snapped. I just wanted it. You said you had some appointment, so I figured you'd drop your stuff off and then you'd be gone. So I went to take it."

A theft Loretta Mae had thwarted by spiriting it away into the attic for safekeeping. Bless you, Meemaw, I thought. Bless you.

Chapter Eighteen

I sat in one of the rocking chairs on my front porch. The other rocked beside me in a steady rhythm. The poem Tawny had on her desk with her brother Christopher's photo came to mind. Meemaw would always be near.

Will half stood, half sat on the railing, his back against one of the vertical porch beams. "Let me get this straight," he said. "You think Sue Ellen's heart episodes were triggered when she saw the name tag?"

I pushed my glasses up the bridge of my nose. "Right. Tawny McVie. I think Sue Ellen had wanted to come clean about Christopher's burial place for a long time. Maybe seeing his sister was a sign. When Tawny slipped the last letter into Sue Ellen's bag at the Arts Center telling her to show up at midnight, I think that's when Sue Ellen decided she couldn't hide it anymore."

"Why now? Why did Tawny start with the letters now, after all these years?" Will asked.

I could only hazard a guess at that. "I think all the old suspicions were stirred up when Sue Ellen first registered for the Arts Center class. Tawny saw the name and something snapped."

Will shifted, crossing his legs in front of him. "Sounds like it triggered something in Sue Ellen, too."

"Exactly. That secret probably ate away at her." I thought about her note to me, hastily scribbled in the seconds before Tawny showed up at her house, before Tawny knew about the dress. *It needs to come out.*

Gracie had been listening, perched on the other side of the railing opposite her father. "I don't understand. Sue Ellen could have just told the sheriff if she wanted to let go of the secret. Why didn't she just do that?"

I'd given this some thought. "I don't think Sue Ellen had gotten that far in her need to be free of it. It would have opened a big ol' can of worms for her." I remembered what Bennett Macaw had said when I'd met him in his office. He and Sue Ellen hadn't wanted to drag their kids through the emotional rollercoaster of a divorce unless they were sure. In my heart, I thought that same motivation propelled Sue Ellen to keep her secret. She wanted to protect her children from the circus the truth would unleash.

The front gate creaked. For a split second, I thought Meemaw had vacated her spot on the rocking chair and was playing jokes, but Mary Lou strode through. She walked up the steps and plopped herself down on the rocking chair. An otherworldly moan seemed to float on the wind. Mary Lou jerked her head up, looking at the ceiling, then at me. "What was that?"

I pasted an innocent expression on my face. "What was what?"

She looked from me to Will to Gracie. "That sound. Did you hear it?"

Will caught my gaze but said, "No."

Gracie's eyes popped open wide, and her mouth formed an O to match, but she shook her head.

Meemaw was really testing the boundaries of the Cassidy secrets. I focused on Mary Lou. "How are you holding up?"

Her whole body trembled. "How am I holding up?" she repeated, and then she sighed. "Not too well. It all feels so surreal. Sue Ellen's gone. They exhumed a body from the ranch. It really is Christopher McVie. Daddy really did bury him there. I just...I can't even believe it."

Will stroked his goatee. I knew his thoughts mirrored mine. Sue Ellen knew the body of the boy she'd loved was buried on her father's ranch. She'd planted and nourished her beloved daisies and she'd held on to the secret for thirty-some-odd years. Her message to me was to let the truth come out.

After a minute of silence to honor Christopher, Gracie spoke. "That lady, Tawny...she didn't kill Mrs. Macaw, right?"

Mary Lou nodded. "She wanted answers. She wanted Sue Ellen to tell her the truth and...and..."

"And Sue Ellen's heart gave out," I finished. "Gavin said she won't be charged with murder but the harassment is a crime."

It was all very sad. A single act—Christopher's accidental fall from a horse—had caused a domino effect, irrevocably impacting so many lives. All I could hope now was that Christopher would get the burial he deserved and that maybe...eventually...Tawny could find peace.

I took Sue Ellen's ring from my pocket and handed it to Mary Lou. She folded her fingers over it and held her closed hand to her heart.

After another long minute, I stood. I needed to walk off the emotions coursing through me. "Tea?" I asked.

They all nodded. "I'll help," Gracie said, pushing off the railing.

I stepped inside and stopped short. Gracie bumped into

me with an *oomph*! A tray with a pitcher of iced tea and four glasses floated in the air, moving toward the front door where we stood. "Meemaw," Gracie whispered.

The air rippled and the translucent shape I could barely make out began to solidify into something recognizable. Meemaw's jeans and plaid shirt became faintly visible, more so than I'd ever seen. I held my breath as her boots—red like my favorite pair—hovered above the floor. Her face and dark blond curls started to take shape.

Behind me, I heard the rattle of the doorknob and the jangle of the bells I hung there to announce customers. "I'll help, too." Mary Lou's voice shot through the house like a foghorn on a silent night and the door flung open behind Gracie and me. Instantly and with a loud pop, Meemaw's form vanished. Whatever invisible force was holding up the tray with its pitcher and glasses also disappeared. The tray wavered and started to drop. I lunged, grabbing it, barely managing to keep it from smashing to the ground. Another split second and the whole kit 'n caboodle would've crashed to the floor. "Meemaw!" I said with a hiss under my breath.

I turned to see Mary Lou standing there, gaping at us. "That was so fast," she said slowly. Suspiciously. "How'd you get the tea ready?"

Gracie giggled nervously. "Harlow never tells her secrets," she said.

We went back to the porch, ghostly crisis averted. Mary Lou glanced over her shoulder to the house again, but all was quiet. She moved to stand near Gracie, a sweating glass of iced tea in hand.

"Will you still sell the ranch?" I asked her.

She frowned. "Good lord, I hope so. Especially now. I don't want anything to do with that place anymore. But the investigation has to happen, and Sue Ellen and Bennett weren't divorced, so he'll inherit her half. The mineral rights, too."

"They could make you a lot of money," I said.

"Maybe." She sighed. "I took down the listing. Right now I can't even think about it. At least now I know why Sue Ellen never wanted to sell."

Right. "But now that the truth is out there, she probably wouldn't care, right? She'd want you to do whatever makes you happy."

"Do you think so?" Mary Lou's voice was laced with hopefulness.

"I do. She was trying to unbury her secret," I said. "Now that it is out in the open, you're free to do whatever you want."

"If Bennett agrees."

We sipped our tea and I rocked while Mary Lou, Gracie, and Will leaned against the porch railing, side by side. "You'll work it out," he said. "I know Bennett Macaw. He's a reasonable man."

I wasn't so sure about that. He definitely had two sides to him—the side I'd seen at the hospital and the side I'd seen at the coffee shop and at his office. But maybe Will was right. For Mary Lou's sake, I hoped so.

Mary Lou pushed off the railing and sank into the vacant rocking chair. "Ohh!"

I spun to look at her. "Are you okay?"

Her expression turned from stunned to peaceful. "That was so strange. The air just turned really warm. Like a blanket wrapped around me."

Meemaw.

"You feel better, right?" Gracie asked.

Mary Lou drew in her brows, considering the question. "I do," she said. "I really think I do.'"

I smiled. Meemaw, bless her heart. She wreaked havoc, but she also worked magic.

That night, after pondering everything that had happened that day, I lay in bed thinking. My charm allowed me to see visions of outfits for people. I'd created a whole new look for Madelyn and it had transformed her from someone who blended into the background to someone who commanded attention. Over and over I'd seen my own magic in action.

When I first met Tawny, I saw her in stripes. Well, polka dots first, then geometric shapes, but the stripes did come. And black and white, to boot, just like the Soggy Bottom Boys from *O Brother, Where Art Thou*. There was definitely more to my charm than I understood and I decided then and there that I needed to figure out how to read between the lines. Maybe then I could prevent murders rather than solve them.

I was still left with one unanswered question, though. "Meemaw," I said into the darkness of my bedroom. "Did Butch Cassidy give me a dark charm? Do I bring about death?"

I held my breath, waiting for her response, but there was none. Only the sheer curtains at my windows lightly fluttered revealing her presence. It was only after my morning shower the next day that I saw her answer written in the steam on the mirror.

Ladybug, your charm is love.

A cocoon of warmth surrounded me and my whole body inflated like a helium balloon being filled with air. Those five little words written by Meemaw's invisible hand had a magical effect on me in a way nothing else ever could. I couldn't say if she knew with utter certainty that my great-great-great-granddaddy's wish hadn't infused me with something dark and outlaw-ish that none of yet understood, but for the moment,

I'd take Meemaw's assurance that whatever else it might be, my charm and everything it represented was mostly about love and not darkness.

"Thanks, Meemaw," I said to the empty room.

Somewhere in the depths of the old farmhouse, the pipes creaked in response. "Love ya, love ya, love ya," they seemed to say.

My heart swelled because my great-grandmother was here with me. "Love ya, too, Loretta Mae Cassidy. Always and forever."

THE END

Every killer has a pattern...

Pleating for Mercy

A MAGICAL DRESSMAKING MYSTERY

"A seamless blend of mystery, magic, and dressmaking."
—JENNIE BENTLEY,
National Bestselling Author

NATIONAL BESTSELLING AUTHOR
MELISSA BOURBON

Start Pleating for Mercy

Chapter 1

Rumors about the Cassidy women and their magic had long swirled through Bliss, Texas, like a gathering tornado. For 150 years, my family had managed to dodge most of the rumors, brushing off the idea that magic infused their handwork, and chalking up any unusual goings-on to coincidence.

But *we* all knew that the magic started the very day Butch Cassidy, my great-great-great-grandfather, turned his back to an ancient Argentinean fountain, dropped a gold coin into it, and made a wish. The Cassidy family legend says he asked for his firstborn child, and all who came after, to live a charmed life, the threads of good fortune, talent, and history flowing like magic from their fingertips.

That magic spilled through the female descendants of the Cassidy line into their handmade tapestries and homespun wool, crewel embroidery, and perfectly pieced and stitched quilts. And into my dressmaking. It connected us to our history, and to each other.

His wish also gifted some of his descendants with their own special charms. Whatever Meemaw, my great-grandmother, wanted, she got. My grandmother Nana was a goat-whisperer. Mama's green thumb could make anything grow.

Yet no matter how hard we tried to keep our magic on the down-low—so we wouldn't wind up in our own contemporary Texas version of the Salem Witch Trials—people noticed. And they talked.

The townsfolk came to Mama when their crops wouldn't grow. They came to Nana when their goats wouldn't behave. And they came to Meemaw when they wanted something so badly they couldn't see straight. I was seventeen when I finally realized that what Butch had really given the women in my family was a thread that connected them with others.

But Butch's wish had apparently exhausted itself before I was born. I had no special charm, and I'd always felt as if a part of me was missing because of it.

Moving back home to Bliss made the feeling stronger.

Meemaw had been gone five months now, but the old red farmhouse just off the square at 2112 Mockingbird Lane looked the same as it had when I was a girl. The steep pitch of the roof, the shuttered windows, the old pecan tree shading the left side of the house—it all sent me reeling back to my childhood and all the time I'd spent here with her.

I'd been back for five weeks and had worked nonstop, converting the downstairs of the house into my own designer dressmaking shop, calling it Buttons & Bows. The name of the shop was in honor of my great-grandmother and her collection of buttons.

What had been Loretta Mae's dining room was now my cutting and workspace. My five-year-old state-of-the-art digital Pfaff sewing machine and Meemaw's old Singer sat side by side on their respective sewing tables. An eight-foot-long white-topped cutting table stood in the center of the room, unused as of yet. Meemaw had one old dress form, which I'd dragged down from the attic. I'd splurged and bought two more, anticipating a brisk dressmaking business, which had yet to materialize.

I'd taken to talking to her during the dull spots in my days. "Meemaw," I said now, sitting in my workroom, hemming a pair of pants, "it's lonesome without you. I sure wish you were here."

A breeze suddenly blew in through the screen, fluttering the butter-yellow sheers that hung on either side of the window as if Meemaw could hear me from the spirit world. It was no secret that she'd wanted me back in Bliss. Was it so far-fetched to think she'd be hanging around now that she'd finally gotten what she'd wanted?

I adjusted my square-framed glasses before pulling a needle through the pants leg. Gripping the thick synthetic fabric sent a shiver through me akin to fingernails scraping down a chalkboard. Bliss was not a mecca of fashion; so far I'd been asked to hem polyester pants, shorten the sleeves of polyester jackets, and repair countless other polyester garments. No one had hired me to design matching mother-and-daughter couture frocks, create a slinky dress for a night out on the town in Dallas, or anything else remotely challenging or interesting.

I kept the faith, though. Meemaw wouldn't have brought me back home just to watch me fail.

As I finished the last stitch and tied off the thread, a flash of something outside caught my eye. I looked past the French doors that separated my workspace from what had been Meemaw's gathering room and was now the boutique portion of Buttons & Bows. The window gave a clear view of the front yard, the wisteria climbing up the sturdy trellis archway, and the street beyond. Just as I was about to dismiss it as my imagination, the bells I'd hung from the doorknob on a ribbon danced in a jingling frenzy and the front door flew open. I jumped, startled, dropping the slacks but still clutching the needle.

A woman sidled into the boutique. Her dark hair was pulled up into a messy but trendy bun and I noticed that her eyes were red and tired-looking despite the heavy makeup she wore. She had on jean shorts, a snap-front top that she'd gathered and tied in a knot below her breastbone, and wedge-heeled shoes. With her thumbs crooked in her back pockets and the way she sashayed across the room, she reminded me of Daisy Duke—with a muffin top.

Except for the Gucci bag slung over her shoulder. That purse was the real deal and had cost more than two thousand dollars, or I wasn't Harlow Jane Cassidy.

A deep frown tugged at the corners of her shimmering pink lips as she scanned the room. "Huh—this isn't at all what I pictured."

Not knowing what she'd pictured, I said, "Can I help you?"

"Just browsing," she said with a dismissive wave. She sauntered over to the opposite side of the room, where a matching olive green and gold paisley damask sofa and loveseat snuggled in one corner. They'd been the nicest pieces of furniture Loretta Mae had owned and some of the few pieces I'd kept. I'd added a plush red velvet settee and a coffee table to the grouping. It was the consultation area of the boutique—though I'd yet to use it.

The woman bypassed the sitting area and went straight for the one-of-a-kind Harlow Cassidy creations that hung on a portable garment rack. She gave a low whistle as she ran her hand from one side to the other, fanning the sleeves of the pieces. "Did you make all of these?"

"I sure did," I said, preening just a tad. Buttons & Bows was a custom boutique, but I had a handful of items leftover from my time in L.A. and New York to display and I'd scrambled to create samples to showcase.

She turned, peering over her shoulder and giving me a once-over. "You don't *look* like a fashion designer."

I pushed my glasses onto the top of my head so I could peer back at her, which served to hold my curls away from my face. Well, *she* didn't look like she could afford a real Gucci, I thought, but I didn't say it. Meemaw had always taught me not to judge a book by its cover. If this woman dragged around an expensive designer purse in little ol' Bliss, she very well might need a fancy gown for something, *and* be able to pay for it.

I balled my fists, jerking when I accidentally pricked my palm with the needle I still held. My smile tightened—from her attitude as well as from the lingering sting on my hand—as I caught a quick glimpse of myself in the freestanding oval mirror next to the garment rack. I looked comfortable and stylish, not an easy accomplishment. Designer jeans. White blouse and color-blocked black-and-white jacket—made by me. Sandals with two-inch heels that probably cost more than this woman's entire wardrobe. Not that I'd had to pay for them, mind you. Even a bottom-of-the-ladder fashion designer employed by Maximilian got to shop at the company's end-of-season sales, which meant fabulous clothes and accessories at a steal. It was a perk I was going to sorely miss.

I kept my voice pleasant despite the bristling sensation I felt creep up inside me. "Sorry to disappoint. What does a fashion designer look like?"

She shrugged, a new strand of hair falling from the clip at the back of her head and framing her face. "Guess I thought you'd look all done up, ya know? Or be a gay man." She tittered.

Huh. She had a point about the gay man thing. "Are you looking for anything in particular? Buttons and Bows is a custom boutique. I design garments specifically for the customer. Other than those items," I said, gesturing to the dresses she was flipping through, "it's not an off-the-rack shop."

Before she could respond, the bells jingled again and the door banged open, hitting the wall. I made a mental note to get a spring or a doorstop. There were a million things to fix around the old farmhouse. The list was already as long as my arm.

A woman stood in the doorway, the bright light from outside sneaking in around her, creating her silhouette. "Harlow Cassidy!" she cried out. "I didn't believe it could really be true, but it is! Oh, thank God! I desperately need your help!"

Read more...

Dear Reader,

I know you have so many choices of books to read. I appreciate you taking the time to read **Bodice of Evidence**.

I love getting up and going to work every day because my characters are so real to me. Living in my imagination is wonderful! Being in Bliss, Texas with Harlow Cassidy and her community is especially fun. I adore her, her people, and the town. When I write this series, I always feel as if I'm visiting friends.

I hope you feel the same. Thanks so much for reading.

Melissa

Read the Entire Series

GET THEM HERE!

Pleating for Mercy

READ THE ENTIRE SERIES

A Fitting End

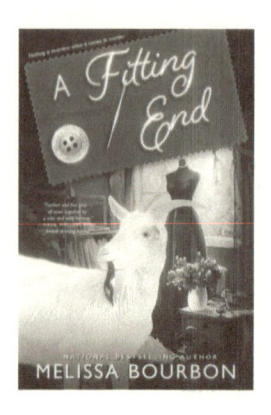

Deadly Patterns

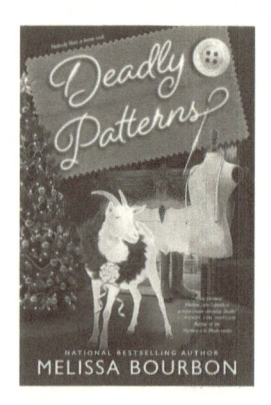

A Custom-Fit Crime

A Killing Notion

READ THE ENTIRE SERIES

A Seamless Murder

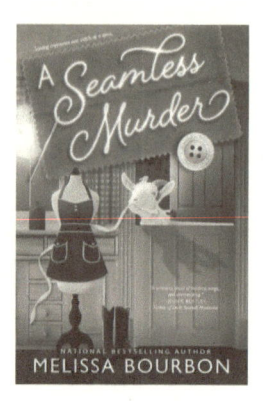

Bobbin for Answers

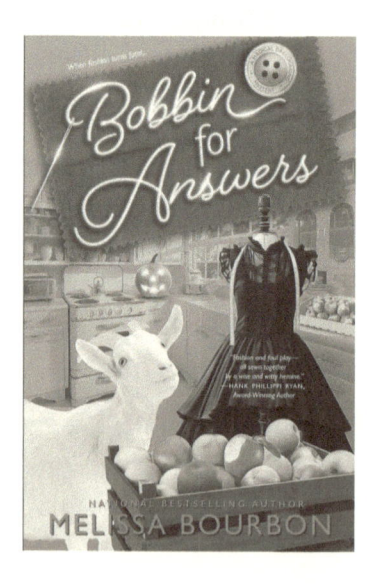

Get more Harlow, Meemaw, and the whole Bliss gang!

About Melissa Bourbon

Melissa Bourbon is the national bestselling author of more than 20 mystery books, including the Lola Cruz Mysteries, A Magical Dressmaking Mystery series, the Bread Shop Mysteries, written as Winnie Archer, and the Book Magic Mysteries.

She is a former middle school English teacher who gave up the classroom in order to live in her imagination full time. Melissa, a California native who has lived in Texas and Colorado, now calls the southeast home. She hikes, practices yoga, cooks, and is slowly but surely discovering all the great restaurants in the Carolinas. Since four of her five amazing kids are living their lives, scattered throughout the country, her dogs, Bean, the pug, Dobby, the chug, and Pippin, the sweet combo, keep her company while she writes.

Melissa lives in North Carolina with her educator husband, Carlos. She is beyond fortunate to be living the life of her dreams.

VISIT Melissa's website at http://www.melissabourbon.com

JOIN her online book club at https://www.facebook.com/groups/BookWarriors/

JOIN her book review club at https://facebook.com/melissaanddianesreviewclub

Books by Melissa

Book Magic Mysteries
The Secret on Rum Runner's Lane
Murder in Devil's Cove
Murder at Sea Captain's Inn
Murder Through an Open Door
Murder and an Irish Curse

Lola Cruz Mysteries
Living the Vida Lola
Hasta la Vista, Lola!
Bare-Naked Lola
What Lola Wants
Drop Dead Lola

Bread Shop Mysteries, *written as Winnie Archer*
Kneaded to Death
Crust No One
The Walking Bread
Flour in the Attic
Dough or Die
Death Gone a-Rye
A Murder Yule Regret
Bread Over Troubled Water

Magical Dressmaking Mysteries
Pleating for Mercy

A Fitting End
Deadly Patterns
A Custom-Fit Crime
A Killing Notion
A Seamless Murder
Bobbin for Answers

Mystery/Suspense
Silent Obsession
Silent Echoes
Deadly Legends Boxed Set

Paranormal Romance
Storiebook Charm